A man we...
the passen...

He reached in to grab the evidence from Kara. She held on. "No. Let go!"

Jeremy pressed the release button on his seat belt, but the mechanism wouldn't unbuckle. He yanked at the strap.

He could slide his weapon from his holster, but there was no way he could fire at the man without risking Kara's safety. He reached for the knife on his utility belt.

The assailant trying to wrest the bat from Kara reared back and punched her in the face.

Her head snapped back. Clearly dazed, Kara moaned. Her eyes closed and she slumped in the seat.

"No!" Jeremy quickly sawed through the seat belt. He had to help her.

Another masked man appeared beside the first one.

"Grab her," he yelled, as he took the evidence and whirled away. The other man reached for Kara.

Jeremy scrambled from his seat to shove his gun into the masked man's face.

Award-winning, multi-published author **Terri Reed** writes heartwarming romance and heart-pounding suspense. Her books have appeared on *Publishers Weekly* top ten, Nielsen BookScan top fifty and Amazon Bestseller lists and featured in *USA TODAY*. When not writing, she can be found doing agility with her dog or digging in her garden. You can visit her online at www.terrireed.com, sign up for her newsletter for exclusive content or email her at terrireedauthor@terrireed.com.

Books by Terri Reed

Love Inspired Suspense

Buried Mountain Secrets
Secret Mountain Hideout
Christmas Protection Detail
Secret Sabotage
Forced to Flee
Forced to Hide
Undercover Christmas Escape
Shielding the Innocent Target
Trained to Protect
Texas Christmas Cover-Up

Pacific Northwest K-9 Unit

Explosive Trail

Mountain Country K-9 Unit

Search and Detect

Dakota K-9 Unit

Standing Watch

Visit the Author Profile page at LoveInspired.com for more titles.

TEXAS CHRISTMAS COVER-UP

TERRI REED

LOVE INSPIRED SUSPENSE
INSPIRATIONAL ROMANCE

If you purchased this book without a cover you should be aware that this book is stolen property. It was reported as "unsold and destroyed" to the publisher, and neither the author nor the publisher has received any payment for this "stripped book."

LOVE INSPIRED® SUSPENSE
INSPIRATIONAL ROMANCE

ISBN-13: 978-1-335-95734-4

Recycling programs for this product may not exist in your area.

Texas Christmas Cover-Up

Copyright © 2025 by Terri Reed

All rights reserved. No part of this book may be used or reproduced in any manner whatsoever without written permission.

Without limiting the author's and publisher's exclusive rights, any unauthorized use of this publication to train generative artificial intelligence (AI) technologies is expressly prohibited.

This is a work of fiction. Names, characters, places and incidents are either the product of the author's imagination or are used fictitiously. Any resemblance to actual persons, living or dead, businesses, companies, events or locales is entirely coincidental.

For questions and comments about the quality of this book, please contact us at CustomerService@Harlequin.com.

® is a trademark of Harlequin Enterprises ULC.

Love Inspired
22 Adelaide St. West, 41st Floor
Toronto, Ontario M5H 4E3, Canada
www.LoveInspired.com

Printed in Lithuania

MIX
Paper | Supporting responsible forestry
FSC® C021394

I am come a light into the world, that whosoever believeth on me should not abide in darkness.
—*John* 12:46

Writing is never done in a void, even though it is a solitary endeavor. Many people have supported and encouraged me through the journey of life and writing. I want to acknowledge a few here:

To Judy Helm, my sister in Christ,
I'm thankful for your friendship and wisdom.

To my critique partner, Leah Vale, as always, I'd be lost in the weeds without you reeling me back in and keeping me on solid ground.

To my editors, Katie Gowrie and Tina James—I'm so thankful for your direction, support and guidance as we work together to make the books shine.

ONE

"This was a bad idea," FBI Special Agent Kara Evans-Mitchell muttered as she brought the rental car to a halt in the driveway of her childhood home. The two-story house was located in a residential neighborhood north of the city center of South Padre Island, Texas.

For some reason, the fine hairs at her nape quivered with tension.

There was no cause for her to be spooked. She shook off the sensation and studied the scene before her.

It was the only house on the block without festive, bright Christmas lights. Instead, it stood dark against the moonlit night except for the glow of a single porch light, illuminating the teal-blue of the exterior, a color synonymous with the island.

She wasn't sure what she'd expected—maybe the grass to be overgrown by weeds and the paint chipped from neglect. But the home where she'd grown up looked, at least in the dark, well cared for. Maintained.

Why had her mother bothered when she'd been adamant she could never return?

And now never would.

Sadness tightened the corners of Kara's eyes as she blinked back the tears. Her mother had passed peacefully at home two weeks ago under the care of a private nurse. Kara had held her mother's hand as she'd left this earthly life. Per her mother's wishes, there was no service. Her mother had wanted to be laid to rest without a fuss.

An emptiness settled over Kara.

She had never understood why her mother hadn't sold the home. It had been over twelve years since they'd left the island and the house behind.

Over twelve years since her father's brutal murder.

Her mother had been frantic to leave, her grief overwhelming, her need to cling to her only child smothering.

Kara barely remembered those first days after the news that her father had been found bludgeoned to death on the high school baseball field.

She'd been distraught, her own grief inconsolable.

The only bright spot had been Jeremy Hamilton. Her father's favorite baseball player and…her boyfriend. He'd been her anchor.

Until he hadn't.

The assault of memories battering her mind had her gripping and re-gripping the steering wheel. She couldn't bring herself to shut off the engine. The urge to bolt was so strong she nearly gave in.

But she knew deep inside she couldn't outrun grief or sorrow.

Still, she wished she'd instructed the real estate agent to box everything up and give it to charity.

But after having her home in Virginia robbed earlier this week, Kara had felt the need for a change of scenery and a sense of closure to process her mom's death. Taking on the task of closing up the old house in Texas had seemed like the perfect escape from the snowy December weather in Virginia. Though now, all she wanted to do was turn around and head for the airport.

Movement from the back seat had her turning off the engine and lifting her hands from the steering wheel.

"Mommy, are we here?"

She twisted in her seat to reach for her four-year-old daughter's hand, petal soft and so trusting. Kara's heart squeezed tight with love. "We're here, honeybee. Give me a sec to get everything ready, and then I'll take you inside."

Squaring her shoulders with resignation and determination to get this over with as soon as possible and head back to Virginia, Kara popped open the driver's-side door and stepped out into the temperate December air.

A chill skated across her flesh.

She frowned. The temperature on the island was in the mid-fifties. Nothing like the arctic blast she'd left back in Alexandria. In the distance, she heard the waves of the Gulf of Mexico rushing onto the sandy shores, a sound she'd fallen asleep to for most of her life. She breathed in the familiar sea-salted air. The beach had been her favorite place, filled with fun and young love.

Shaking off the nostalgia worming its way into her consciousness, she popped open the trunk and removed her and Emily's bags. They were only staying for two nights, so she'd packed light.

Maybe only one night, if she could quickly find the documents she needed. Changing their scheduled flight back wouldn't be a problem. She'd pay whatever fee was necessary. Then she'd hire movers to pack everything up and take it all to the donation bin for the local church. She didn't need anything from this house except her mother's will, which Kara hadn't been able to find in her mother's possession in

Virginia. As well as needing the mortgage documents so she could put the house on the market.

Glancing up and down the suburban neighborhood on the north side of South Padre Island, she smiled at all the holiday-decorated yards: Blow-up reindeer and Santas. A colorful nativity scene across the street. Christmas trees shining brightly through front windows.

All was quiet. Most people were tucked in for the night, either watching television or already asleep. Her gaze traveled to the moon. The round orb bathed the world in a soft glow.

She closed her eyes, envisioning the path she used to take to Jeremy's house, only a few blocks away.

She wondered if his parents still lived there. Or had they moved?

Probably moved. That had to be the reason their number had been disconnected all those years ago.

She shook off the questions and the melancholy that descended.

Jeremy was her distant past. Emily was her future.

It was time to firmly close this chapter of her life. And maybe even close the chapter of their lives in Alexandria. Now that her mother had passed on, Kara could sell that house too and move to somewhere fresh. She made a mental note to start searching for their new home as soon as she finished up here. With the work she did for the FBI, she could live anywhere that had an FBI office.

She carried the bags to the front porch and set them down at her feet. Using the key she still had on her key fob, she unlocked and opened the front door.

The dark interior yawned like a cavernous abyss.

A musty odor hit her nostrils, making her nose wrinkle. No doubt a layer of dust would cover everything. Maybe she and Emily should go to a hotel tonight. It might be for the best.

On the verge of retreating, the scrape of a shoe on hardwood set off her internal alarm system to a blaring roar.

Someone was in the house.

Reflexively, she reached for her sidearm beneath her lightweight blazer.

Glancing over her shoulder and assuring herself Emily was still safely strapped in her car seat within the confines of the car, Kara sent up a silent prayer for protection.

If the house had a squatter, Kara needed to deal with it quietly and efficiently. Calling the police was not an option. She didn't want Officer Jeremy Hamilton showing up on her doorstep.

She needed to keep a low profile. Get in and out of town without any fuss or drama.

Or any more heartache.

She thumbed the lock on the rental-car key chain, locking Emily inside. With her daughter secure in the car, Kara moved into the inky darkness.

Her hand hovered over the wall light switch. She debated filling the house with the overhead lights and then decided against it.

Better to have surprise on her side.

As it was, the ambient light of the moon spilled in through the open front door, allowing her to move deeper into the living room and head for the kitchen. Muscle memory had her skirting around an end table that stuck out into the path. As a kid, she'd hit that table more times than she could count.

A shadow darker than the dimness of the house's interior appeared in her line of sight from the hallway to her right.

A shadow in the form of a man.

She whirled toward the shape, drawing her weapon. "Halt! FBI."

Though she had no jurisdiction here on the local level, her badge would be enough to scare any squatter away.

For half a second, the intruder paused, and then, instead of running for the door, he rushed her, swiping the unlit lamp off the end table and swinging it in her direction.

The brass base of the lamp hit her hand with a stinging crack, sending her weapon flying from her grasp.

The hard *thunk* of the metal weapon hitting the hardwood floor and skittering away echoed through her brain.

She needed to get her gun.

She dove to the side, landing on her stomach as her cheek slammed against the smooth surface of the hardwood floor. Ignoring the burst of pain, she reached for the grip of her Glock.

Her fingertips barely touched the edge of the gun before the intruder wrapped his hands around her ankles and dragged her away from her weapon.

Panic exploded in her chest. Despite bucking and kicking, her efforts to make the man release his hold proved ineffective.

Fear and fury mingled, fueling her determination to break free. Her training kicked in.

Twisting to her back, she curled and forcefully drew her knees up, bringing the assailant closer. She leveraged her feet onto his hip while covering her head to ward off his fist. With a burst of power, she shoved her feet into his hips, causing him to loosen his hold on her right foot enough for her to yank her ankle from his grasp.

Liberated from his hold, she kicked with all her might, the bottom of her short, heeled boot striking the man square in the chest.

With an *oof*, he let go of her.

Freed from his grip, she scrambled to retrieve her sidearm.

The assailant blasted to his feet and took off running.

Pushing to her knees, she aimed her weapon at the retreating back of the intruder as he raced out the front door and passed beneath the porch light.

Her assailant wasn't a homeless person seeking shelter but rather a masked man. What was he doing in her home?

Jumping to her feet, she sped out of the house. The man pounded the pavement down the street and turned the corner.

Should she chase after him?

No. Her steps faltered, and she slowed. She needed to protect her child. A quick glance toward her rental car reassured her that Emily was protected in the back seat.

Moments later, the sound of an engine filled the night air, and then the roar of a car driving away let her know going after the intruder would be futile.

Adrenaline pumped through Kara's veins, causing ragged breathing. Shaking, she holstered her weapon and headed to the car.

Lights came on in the house next door. An older couple she'd never seen before stepped out on their front porch. The husband took a protective stance near his wife. "We've called the police."

Kara's stomach sank but she waved an acknowledgment to the new neighbors. She just hoped and prayed that Jeremy wasn't on duty tonight. The last thing she needed was to come face-to-face with the man who'd broken her heart.

Her gaze turned to the undecorated house. Why was a stranger in her childhood home, and what had he been after?

A shudder worked over her.

Worse yet, would he return?

Crime scene tape cordoned off the area beneath the boardwalk attached to Beach Park, one of South Padre Island's amusement parks. The yellow-and-black bands flapped in the slight breeze coming in off the ocean. Police Chief Jeremy Hamilton stood with his arms crossed as he stared down at the third murder victim to be found in his jurisdiction in less than a week.

His gut churned with acid.

Were the murders connected, or was this a coincidence?

He didn't believe in coincidence. Everything happened for a reason, even if the reason was known only to God.

"Rodgers says looks like the same MO," Officer Tarren McGregor said as he and his K-9, Raz, a dark-colored German shepherd, moved to stand next to Jeremy.

Rodgers was the department's homicide detective by way of the New York Police Department. When Jeremy had become chief, he'd recruited experienced officers to their small department.

"My thoughts exactly." As with the other two victims, this one had been shot in the chest and there was bruising on the face, indicating the man had taken a beating before being killed. Having three murders with the same modus operandi wasn't good for the island.

Even though it was December, plenty of tourists wanting a tropical Christmas experience filled the hotels and vacation homes. It was Jeremy's job to make sure everyone stayed safe.

"We'll see what the medical examiner has to say." Jeremy pushed back the brim of his tan cowboy hat and scanned the deserted area.

Sand stretched for miles to the north and the south. Waves rushed up the shoreline and retreated again. Because it was after hours for the park, this section of the beach was quiet as usual, though the more popular beaches near the resorts would still have swimmers in the temperate waters.

"The victim was dumped," Tarren replied. "There's no blood pooling in the sand beneath him."

"We have our work cut out for us. Again." Frustration reverberated through Jeremy, seeping into his words.

Like the other two murdered victims, the body had been dumped at a secondary crime scene. They had yet to find the primary scene of the crime for any of the victims.

The radio on Jeremy's shoulder crackled to life and a dispatcher's voice came through. "Chief, we have reports of an intruder at the Evans home."

Jeremy's heart bumped against his ribs.

He knew the address by heart. He'd spent a lot of time there from age eleven through seventeen, until his world derailed with the murder of his mentor and baseball coach.

The horror of learning the details of Coach Paul Evans's bludgeoned body laid out on the home plate of the high school baseball field would forever be etched into his brain.

"You want me to take it?" Tarren asked.

Jeremy appreciated his best friend's sensitivity. Tarren had been just as close to Coach Evans.

Only Jeremy had also been dating the coach's daughter, Kara.

Jeremy was tempted to relinquish the responsibility of responding to the call over to Tarren. But they were both on duty tonight. There was nothing more they could do at this site. Rodgers had it in hand. Forensics were on the scene, and the ME was on the way.

"We'll both go."

Tarren nodded.

Jeremy was thankful that his best friend and best officer didn't remark on the fact that they were headed to Jeremy's ex-girlfriend's abandoned home.

When Kara Evans and her mother, Laine Evans, left town

over twelve years ago, there had been promises made between Kara and Jeremy.

Promises that had been broken.

Neither Kara nor Laine had returned to the island in all that time, yet for some reason Laine had kept up the house, making sure the yard was always tended to once a week. For years the fact she'd that had someone maintain the place had given Jeremy hope that they would return.

That Kara would return.

But that hope had died.

And in order to move forward, he'd squashed his feelings for Kara.

Still, he was the chief of police for South Padre Island and he had a job to do. A job that included protecting the property that belonged to his deceased beloved coach and mentor.

After giving instructions to the other officers on the scene to contain the area and wait for the medical examiner, Jeremy climbed into his official South Padre Island Police Department vehicle.

Tarren and Raz went to their new vehicle, a state-of-the-art K-9 SUV, thanks to the grateful rich parents of a teenager who'd been rescued by Tarren and Raz. Their previous vehicle had been destroyed last year when the teenager had been kidnapped.

With Jeremy leading the way, they drove from the amusement park through the festively decorated downtown and then the more residential area.

Normally, Jeremy bypassed the Evanses' street to head to his parents' house. But tonight, as he made the turn, it felt strangely familiar and odd at the same time. The house, midway down the block and undecorated for the holiday season, was lit up, as well as the house next door.

An older couple Jeremy recognized as Olivia and Larry

Bauman met him as soon as he parked behind a blue sedan in the Evanses' driveway.

Jeremy only half listened to the couple as his gaze zeroed in on the brunette woman sitting on the porch holding a young child on her lap.

His heart expanded and then retracted painfully within his chest.

Kara Evans was the intruder?

Kara kept her daughter wrapped in her arms and secure on her lap as they waited on the porch for the South Padre Island police to arrive. She saw the vehicles pull up, one parking behind her rental and the other at the curb.

Dropping her gaze to her daughter's trusting eyes, she murmured, "Everything's going to be fine, honeybee. Mommy's got you."

Emily snuggled closer.

The sound of the older couple relaying to the police how they'd seen the woman arrive and then a masked man run out of the house had Kara's nerves stretched taut.

At the low rumble of a familiar male voice, everything inside of her tightened.

It couldn't be Jeremy, could it?

Heart thundering, she kept her gaze lowered.

As a federal agent, she normally would have stopped in at a police department to inform them of her presence. But she wasn't here on official business. This was personal. So she hadn't made that courtesy visit at this late hour.

She felt rather than heard someone approaching. Felt the presence of someone standing in front of her.

Slowly, she allowed her gaze to land on the black steel-toed boots that had stopped two feet from her. Her gaze traveled up the dark slacks and tan uniform shirt of the South Padre

Island police force, snagging on the nameplate attached to the breast pocket of the shirt pulled taut across a muscled chest.

She sucked in a sharp breath.

Her gaze lifted and met the green-gold gaze of Jeremy Hamilton.

Even though his tan cowboy hat shaded his face, she'd recognize him anywhere. A realization came to her in a flash as embarrassment rushed to her cheeks.

Not only was Jeremy on the police force, he was the police chief. And there was no way she was getting out of the situation without more heartache.

TWO

Why hadn't Kara known that Jeremy was the police chief of South Padre Island? She silently scoffed to herself. She hadn't wanted to know the details of Jeremy's life after he'd ghosted her all those years ago. She'd only learned he'd joined the police force from her uncle on one of his visits.

Jeremy was most likely married and had children of his own by now.

Why did the thought stir up a seed of jealousy?

Her arms tightened around her daughter.

Emily squirmed. "Mommy, too tight."

With a sigh, she loosened her hold and rose to her feet, positioning Emily on her hip.

She was thankful to be on the second-to-the-top stair, which made her eye level with Jeremy.

He stared at her, his gaze never wavering. The only sign of emotion was the slight tick in the side of his strong, squared jaw.

"You have a daughter," he murmured. "Is she okay?"

The tight tone of his voice slid over her, prickling her skin. "We're fine. This is Emily."

His expression softened. "Hi, Emily. I'm Jeremy. An old friend of your mother's."

An old friend. If only it was that simple.

Movement behind him snagged her attention. Past Jeremy's shoulder, another man approached along with a beautiful German shepherd.

Pleasant surprise had her smiling. "Tarren, is that you?"

The tall, lanky teen she remembered had become a very handsome, muscular man.

Just like the man standing in front of her, not saying a word. But she wasn't ready to deal with him.

"Hey, Kara," Tarren said.

"So, you're the intruder."

Jeremy's deep voice reverberated through her. Her gaze jumped back to his. She bristled against the challenge in both his tone and the arch of his eyebrow. "No, actually. In case you've forgotten, this is my house."

He gave a slow nod. "I'll make sure the neighbors know everything is okay."

Kara gritted her teeth. She didn't want to tell him, but she needed to. "Actually, there was an intruder. The house has been ransacked."

That made him blink. His eyes narrowed. "Who knew you were coming here?"

Under the spotlight of the porch lamp outside her childhood home, Kara lifted her chin. Annoyance swamped her as she stared Jeremy down. "Are you really going to blame me for this?"

His lips twitched. A frown dipped between his brows. "Just seems a little odd that the night you show up there's a break-in. The house has sat uninhabited for twelve years without any problems. Seems suspicious."

She disliked that what he said was true. "Odd isn't the word I'd use. More like disturbing." And she hated to contemplate what the break-ins could mean.

But she was a realist. Something was going on, and she was going to have to deal with it.

However, that didn't mean she needed Jeremy.

A frown darkened his handsome face. "How so?"

Shifting her daughter on her hip, she glanced at the curious neighbors standing on the sidewalk. She reined in the flare of temper threatening to bust loose. "Can we take this inside?"

Jeremy inhaled a noisy breath. Obviously, he struggled to keep his cool as well.

For a second, they were twelve again, vying for the pitcher's spot. Her dad, the coach and consummate peacemaker, had settled the conflict by having them rotate with each batter.

After a beat, Jeremy stepped onto the porch, towering over her before moving past her without a word. He entered the house, stopping so that he blocked the doorway.

She made a face at his back. "Are you going to let us in?"

He turned but didn't budge. "This is now a crime scene. I'll have the forensic team come here as soon as they're done at another location, and they'll dust for prints. In the morning, we'll come back so you can determine if anything is missing."

Her heart sank. She should have gone straight to a hotel when she arrived in town. Then at least she'd be facing him with a clear mind after a good night's sleep. She doubted she'd find any rest tonight now. "Fine."

She turned on her heel and marched back to the rental car. Before she could reach and open the back-seat door, he was there.

The South Padre Island police chief moved with grace and stealth.

"What are you doing back here, Kara?" There was no mistaking his curiosity or the tension in his tone. His gaze bounced to Emily.

Feeling cranky and upset, she said, "It's a free country. Now, step aside, Chief."

He remained in place. A wall of man between her and the car. "Where will you go?"

His gentle tone made her regret her earlier sharpness. "One of the resorts on the beach. I'll make sure your office has all my contact information."

"Boss." Tarren stepped over and gestured to Jeremy that he wanted to talk. For a moment, Kara didn't think Jeremy would heed his officer's signal as he continued to stare at her.

Finally, Jeremy gave a nod. "Don't go anywhere. I'll be right back."

He stepped away to join Tarren. The two conversed in hushed tones.

Since his vehicle was blocking her car, what choice did she have but to wait for him? She turned her back on the pair and secured her daughter in her car seat in the back of the rental.

"I'm hungry, Mommy," Emily groused.

"We'll get a snack soon, sweetie." It had been several hours since they'd eaten on the plane.

Rubbing her eyes, Emily said, "Sleepy."

"Me, too. You can close your eyes for a bit." Kara was grateful Emily hadn't had a meltdown. But if she didn't get to bed soon, she might.

A moment later, Jeremy returned. She straightened and closed the car door.

"Tarren will secure the scene and wait for the forensic techs."

Unsure why he was telling her this, she nodded because that seemed like the right thing to do. "Can you move your vehicle?"

"You have a bruise forming on your face."

Reflexively, she touched her cheek, which made her aware

of the throbbing from where she'd hit the hardwood floor. But she had other issues on her mind besides the aches and pains of grappling with the intruder.

"I don't think this was some random act, Kara," Jeremy said, his tone concerned. "You said this was disturbing. Are you in some kind of trouble?"

Her defenses rose again. "Why would you think this is my fault?" she shot back even though worry quaked through her.

Had she done something recently to attract the unwanted attention of a criminal?

During the course of her work as a profiler for the FBI, she'd rubbed many people, both law enforcement and civilians, the wrong way, as well as being instrumental in bringing a number of suspects to justice. So sure, she could have enemies. But here in South Padre Island? Doubtful.

"I'm not saying you're at fault." His tone was measured.

She sucked in a breath. He was handling her. She didn't like it. She didn't need to be coddled. Considering someone had robbed her home in Alexandria earlier in the week, trouble could have followed her. But the timing was off. No one had known she was headed home to South Padre Island except her boss and a few close friends.

Jeremy touched her hand, a soft caress that sent her senses reeling.

She tucked her hands behind her back.

He held up his palms in surrender. "I'd feel more comfortable if I could take you and—" he ducked his head to look at Emily through the window before straightening "—your daughter to my parents' house. There's plenty of room there. Then you and I can chat."

"A hotel will do."

His eyebrows dipped into a frown. "Kara, it's late. I'm

sure your daughter is scared enough and could use a warm, welcoming place to sleep."

The Hamiltons weren't strangers to her. At one time, Kara had hoped to be a part of their family. And she knew Emily would love them.

Kara mentally stepped back from the situation.

She needed to look at this analytically and form a plan. What he was suggesting was sound. Being in a home rather than a sterile hotel room would be more comforting for Emily. Kara knew that Jeremy's parents, both of whom were doctors, would dote on her little girl.

A sudden yearning welled up inside of her. She'd missed the Hamilton family. Irene and Rick Hamilton had always been welcoming to Kara, even though they both worked long hours. And Julia, Jeremy's sister, had been such a dear friend.

Kara and Emily could both use a bit of comforting. "Do your parents live in the same house?"

Jeremy cocked his head. "They do."

"But they changed their phone number," she said, thinking back to the last time she'd tried to call Jeremy's house and had received the metallic voice saying the number was no longer in service.

Surprise flared in his eyes. "They did a long time ago. They were receiving prank calls and decided the best solution was to get a new number."

What he said made sense. Anxiety bubbled up. "Are you sure they'll be okay with this?"

Maybe her memories of the Hamiltons' kindness were faulty. Maybe they, like their son, had been glad to see her leave town.

"My parents will be happy to see you."

One corner of his mouth lifted in a half smile, and her heart gave a little thump in her chest.

She bit back the stirring of attraction. There was no way she was going to allow herself to be drawn in by Jeremy Hamilton ever again.

Especially not when she and her daughter might be in danger.

I don't think this was some random act.

She didn't, either. But she had no clue as to why someone would ransack both of her homes.

And the unknown factor left her uneasy.

For her daughter's sake, she was willing to trust Jeremy with their safety, but that was it. "We'll follow you to your parents'."

Jeremy called his parents on the way from the Evanses' house to let them know they were coming. His parents had been full of questions he couldn't answer.

Tarren and Raz had stayed behind to wait for the forensic team.

Driving slowly through the holiday-decorated neighborhoods, Jeremy kept an eye on the headlights of Kara's car behind him, while giving himself and his parents time to process the fact that Kara Evans was back in town.

And she'd come with a child.

A child that was a mini version of Kara, with the same dark hair and violet-hued blue eyes. Even if the little girl hadn't called Kara *Mommy*, he would have known she was Kara's.

Was she married? He hadn't noticed a ring. Where was Emily's father?

Jeremy had so many things he wanted to ask her. Things about the past. Things about the present.

But he needed to stay focused on the here and now. Why

had somebody ransacked her home the same night she arrived? Had the intruder been waiting for her?

No, that didn't make sense. If the assailant had been there to hurt Kara... The thought sent a shudder through him.

The masked man clearly was searching for something. But what? And why now?

It was a puzzle, one he was determined to solve.

And he would stay professional and not give in to the emotions crowding through his chest. He tamped down the attraction, the resentment and the affection with practiced ease.

When it came to Kara Evans, he knew better than to ever let down his walls again.

The woman had walked out of his life without a backward glance.

A whisper of reason had him admitting that statement wasn't entirely true.

They had emailed each other for a short time, but then she'd stopped answering. Until out of the blue, she'd sent an email asking him to stop writing, claiming he was a painful reminder of the loss of her father.

He'd printed her replies and kept them as a reminder to never let anyone get close enough again to break his heart.

Caging the betrayal behind the invisible barricade of protection he'd erected around his heart, he parked at the curb in front of his childhood home and allowed Kara to park in the driveway.

He noted the rental sticker on the bumper. How long was she planning to stay? And why had she come back? Did she still work for the FBI?

Last he'd heard, she was a profiler with an impressive record.

Knowing he would get the answers in due time, he climbed out of his vehicle and took the two bags from the trunk of Kara's car while she lifted her child from the back seat. He led the way to the front door of the two-story beachfront home.

White icicle lights hung from the eaves. A green wreath sporting a red bow hung on the front door, and a large Christmas tree twinkled in the front window. His mom loved this time of year with all its festive trimmings. She always made the holidays special.

Before they reached the front door, it swung open. His mother and father filled the frame.

Irene Hamilton smiled, the soft wrinkles around her green eyes the only real signs she was nearly seventy. She was tall and slender, with blond hair loose about her slim shoulders. "Kara, it's so good to see you. Who is this little one?"

"I'm Emily," the little girl said before ducking her head into the curve of her mother's neck.

"Well, hello, Emily, I'm Irene and this is Rick," his mother said as she patted her husband on the chest. "We're so excited you're going to stay the night with us."

"That we are," Rick said. "Kara, it's been a long time. Please, come in."

"Thank you," Kara murmured as she carried Emily into the house.

Jeremy moved to follow, but his father blocked the doorway.

"Let the ladies settle in," Rick said and motioned for Jeremy to step farther onto the porch with him.

Setting the bags near the door, Jeremy moved to stand beside his father.

Rick Hamilton was a big, strong man with broad shoulders and a full head of silver hair. One would never look at him and think *heart surgeon*. "From what you said, I gather Kara and her daughter are in danger."

Jeremy nodded. "Someone broke into their family home

and ransacked the place. The intruder was there when Kara arrived."

"Well, that must have been terrifying. I'm glad you brought them here."

Kara had appeared unfazed. As a profiler for the FBI, she was probably good at hiding her emotions, a skill many in law enforcement mastered.

"I'll be staying the night as well," Jeremy stated.

Dad's eyebrows rose. "This must be serious."

"I don't know yet," Jeremy told him. "But until I have a better grasp of what's happening, I'll be protecting Kara and her daughter."

In the glow of the porch light, his dad's expression turned pensive. "Hard to protect them well if you don't know what you're protecting them from."

A true statement. "As I said, Dad, I intend to find out what's going on."

Dad clapped him on the back. "What an interesting reunion."

"Understatement," Jeremy muttered as they entered the house and shut the door behind them.

The living room looked like a Christmas store had thrown up. Every available space had some sort of decoration. Most he recognized, but every year his mother added to her Christmas collection.

Jeremy found the ladies in the kitchen. His mom, wearing a red-and-white-striped apron, stood at the stove making hot cocoa with real milk and melted chunks of chocolate. A bag of mini marshmallows sat on the counter next to the stove. His mom's hot chocolate with marshmallows was one of his and his sister's favorite treats.

Emily was seated on a stool at the counter, munching on shortbread cookies.

Kara stood protectively beside her.

For a moment, Jeremy was transported back to high school when Kara had been a fixture in their home. Life had seemed so simple then, their path forward so clear. A path that had included attending the same college, getting married and having a family.

He'd had dreams then of playing college baseball with hopes of a professional career.

But life had taken a sharp turn with the coach's death and Kara's departure from his life.

The old wound of her abandonment cracked open.

When Kara and her mom left town, they didn't just leave Jeremy behind but everyone else who had loved them.

Taking off his cowboy hat, he set it on the bench in the dining room before saying, "Kara, could we step out back?"

She met his gaze. Her eyes were still the same lovely purple-blue hue that had slayed him when they were kids.

With a nod, she put an arm around her daughter's shoulder and leaned in to kiss her cheek. "I'll be right outside if you need me."

"Okay, Mommy," Emily said around a mouthful of shortbread.

With a tender smile softening her features, Kara turned back to Jeremy.

He felt a kick in the chest. How often had he dreamed of seeing her again?

Too often for his peace of mind.

Abruptly, he turned on his heel and headed out through the sliding glass door to the expansive porch beyond. The lights of the heated kidney-shaped pool illuminated the clear water. He stepped to the edge where the cement met the swath of grass that separated the property from the beach. He lifted his gaze upward to stare at the nearly full moon.

Kara joined him. "You have questions."

So many. Where to start? "What brings you back to South Padre Island?"

"My mother's death," she said in a matter-of-fact tone.

Empathy flooded his veins. He turned to face her.

She stared out at the ocean.

"I'm sorry to hear of your loss. What happened?"

"Colon cancer." Though her voice was steady, now there was an undertone of sadness. He wanted to take her into his arms. Instead, he jammed his hands into his pockets.

"I need to sell the house," she continued. "I buried her two weeks ago."

"That's rough." He didn't even want to contemplate the passing of his own parents. "Was she sick for long?"

Turning her face up to the moon, she shrugged. "Depends on what you consider long. The doctors discovered the cancer, stage four, six months ago." She took a deep breath and let it out. "My mom was stubborn. She must have been in pain for a long time, but she refused to go to the doctor."

Jeremy had seen his fair share of stubborn people unwilling to do what was necessary for their health. Sometimes they ended up needing help from emergency responders.

As the police chief, he was always aware of what was happening in his town.

He studied Kara's profile. Same straight nose, high cheekbones and full lips. How many times had he dreamed of that face? "Why do you think someone ransacked your family home? What were they looking for?"

"I've no idea. There's nothing of value that I can think of in the house except maybe the deed or the mortgage. I couldn't find them among my mother's things. The next logical place to look would be here."

"Even if someone stole those documents, they couldn't do

anything with them," he observed as he tried to puzzle out the motive behind the break-in. "There has to be something worth stealing."

"Honestly, I have no idea what was left behind when my mother moved us." She pressed her lips together and then faced him. "But someone didn't just ransack this house. Two weeks ago, my home in Alexandria was also broken into."

The news hit Jeremy like a blast of cold water. "What?"

"They hit my house the same night my mother passed," she said. "At the time, I chalked it up to a string of robberies that had happened in the Alexandria area. They did take some of my mother's jewelry and a couple of pieces of art that I had collected."

Worry for Kara and her daughter tore through him. "Where's Emily's father? Could he be the one doing this?"

Kara heaved a sigh that Jeremy felt in his bones.

"David was killed on the job."

A fresh wave of sympathy crashed over him. He rubbed a hand through his hair to keep from reaching for her. "Kara, I'm sorry..."

He was at a loss for any other words of condolence.

First her father had been murdered. Then she'd lost her husband in the line of duty. And now her mother had passed away. How did she maintain her sanity through so much loss?

"I appreciate your sentiment." Her voice was devoid of emotion. "But right now, I'm more concerned about my daughter's safety. We'll head back to Alexandria first thing in the morning."

Jeremy stared at her, taking in the stubborn jut of her jaw and the tense way she held her shoulders. She seemed so strong, yet he sensed it was an act.

But what did he know?

They were strangers now.

He couldn't let her leave town, though. Not until he got to the bottom of what was going on. "I promise you I will figure out what's happening and keep you and your daughter safe."

Her lush mouth twisted. "Don't make promises you don't intend to keep, Chief."

Her words sliced into him like a knife to the chest. "I'm not the one who broke our promise."

She made a noise in her throat. "Doesn't matter anymore. The past is gone. We can't do anything about it."

Old resentments rose, and he stepped back. She was right. "But I can do something about what's happening now. And I'm asking you not to leave until we figure out why someone is targeting you."

For a long moment, she stared at him.

He could see the wheels turning behind her beautiful eyes. He held his breath. If she refused to stay, there was nothing he could do to stop her.

Besides, she was FBI. She had more resources at her fingertips than he did, which could work to his advantage. "Combining our resources will make this process faster."

She tilted her head. "Even after all this time you still have the uncanny ability to know what I'm thinking."

Surprise had him chuckling. She was so far off base. He'd never known what she was thinking. But if her believing they were on the same page would allow him to help her, then so be it.

And he didn't want to look at why he felt compelled to be the one to protect her and her daughter.

This was his island. And as long as someone in his charge was in danger, he would do everything in his power to keep them safe.

He could handle the physical danger. No sweat. He was trained to meet any situation head on. But could he handle the threat to his heart?

THREE

The sound of Jeremy's low, amused laugh erupted as he watched Emily's animated actions. The little girl was busy telling Jeremy's parents some story as they all gathered around the kitchen counter to sip hot cocoa and nibble on Irene's homemade cookies. The sound and warmth of the moment triggered a memory for Kara.

Watching the tableau and being so close to Jeremy, Kara was transported back to her first real date.

With Jeremy.

Most of the guys in high school hadn't wanted to go near the daughter of the baseball coach. But from the beginning, Jeremy had been different.

They had gone to prom together her junior year. They'd ended up back at his parents' house for an after-party with their friends. It had been the most magical night.

Despite the rivalry between them for her father's attention, she had fallen in love with Jeremy that night. Or maybe it had been that day two weeks earlier when he'd stood up for her against the rest of the baseball team who had wanted to oust the only girl on the team.

Jeremy had told the other players in no uncertain terms that if they couldn't handle having her as a teammate, they should just leave the team.

None left.

Even back then he'd been in command and in charge. The boys had begrudgingly accepted her.

Her heart had become so tangled up in him in unexpected ways.

She must've really been exhausted to allow her thoughts to go backward.

What had her therapist said? Rehashing the past only led to discontentment in the present. Maybe.

But also revisiting the past brought to mind mistakes she would not repeat.

Like falling back into the trap of Jeremy's charm.

She needed to be careful. It wasn't just her heart on the line but her daughter's, too.

Besides, he'd probably given his heart to someone else. So the point was moot.

Jeremy's suggestion that they use their combined resources to discover why someone had broken into both of her homes was logical. His promise to help her...on one hand made her very grateful, yet, on the other hand, unnerved.

She didn't know if she could trust him.

Trust was earned. Could they start fresh?

It was true he'd broken promises to her. Promises that had been made by a seventeen-year-old hormonal teenager. He was a man now.

A respected police chief. That had to account for something.

And frankly, she would rather have the support than go this alone. For her daughter's sake, of course.

"I'd only planned on staying two nights." She turned her attention beyond the patch of grass to watch the waves rolling up to the sand. The sight stirred more memories of playing in the water with friends and Jeremy.

Always Jeremy.

"It might take longer," he said, breaking through her thoughts.

Giving herself a mental shake, she focused on the feel of the salted air on her face. Not something she experienced in Alexandria. Her home was in the suburbs, too far from the water.

"We'll cross that bridge when we come to it." A silence stretched. She fought the urge to fidget. She glanced his way. "Don't you have someone waiting for?"

The lights from the pool played across his face, revealing his devastating grin.

Her heart thumped.

"Are you fishing?"

"What?" She made a scoffing noise, even though that was exactly what she had been doing. "I'm just thinking you don't need to stay here. I'm sure you have somebody waiting for you at your home…which is where?"

His grin widened. "Not married. Nobody is waiting for me. I live downtown."

The news rocked her back a step. And it was on the tip of her tongue to ask *why* he didn't have someone at home waiting for him. Had he lost a spouse as well? Or had he never married? And if not, why?

She bit the words back. It was none of her business.

"In the morning, we will go back to your house." His grin faded, to be replaced by his police-chief persona. He had the whole professional mask down pat. "By then the forensic team will be done dusting for prints. I'll help you look for the documents you need. And we can see if anything obvious is missing."

Fatigue pulled at her. It had been a long day. An emotional roller coaster. She didn't have it in her at the moment to resist his offer of help. "All right. Now, if you don't mind, I'm going to say good-night."

"Good night, Kara."

She left him standing there in the moonlight. But she could feel his gaze on her, and it took effort not to turn around.

Going back to what they'd once had wasn't going to happen, no matter how much her heart ached to do just that.

The next morning, Kara dressed Emily in one of the cute little Christmas outfits that she'd insisted on packing. The white tights with little Christmas trees and the green-and-red-plaid skirt with a ruffled top had become Emily's favorite lately.

Downstairs, the dining room table was set with five place settings. In the middle of the table sat a tray filled with slices of mango, pineapple and strawberries. There was a pitcher of orange juice and a stack of pancakes and warmed syrup waiting to be eaten.

Jeremy rose from his seat at the table. He wore a fresh uniform with neat creases down the pant legs. She supposed he kept a change of clothes in his vehicle or at his parents'. He was so handsome with his light brown—almost sandy blond—hair brushed back off his tanned forehead. His eyes were guarded as he met her gaze.

Learning that he was not married had affected her way more than it should have. All night she'd pondered what his life had been like over the years.

"Emily, do you like pancakes?" Jeremy asked.

"Yes, sir," Emily said shyly.

"May I lift you into the chair?" Though he had directed the question to Emily, his gaze slanted to Kara. He pulled out a chair with a booster seat on it.

Tenderness spread through Kara at the thoughtful gesture. "Where did the booster seat come from?"

"Mom occasionally babysits the neighbors' grandchild."

"Nice." She nodded.

But he waited for Emily to give him permission. Kara's heart melted in a puddle. She hadn't expected him to be so... She couldn't find the right words.

Sweet. Sensitive to her child's feelings. Adorable with the eager expression on his face.

All of the above.

"Yes, sir." Emily held up her arms.

Seeing her daughter trusting Jeremy so freely set Kara's heart pounding.

Jeremy easily lifted Emily off the ground and placed her on the booster seat. He smoothed back a lock of dark hair that had fallen forward. "You can call me Jeremy."

"Yes, Jeremy," Emily said with a giggle.

Seeing her daughter happy had Kara smiling, too.

Grinning, Jeremy pulled out the chair next to Emily for Kara. A shiver of awareness rippled over her skin as she sat. He'd always had good manners. His mother and father had seen to that. But there was something almost intimate about his gentlemanly ways that had her feeling both at home and uncomfortable.

Jeremy rounded the table and sat on the other side of Emily. He forked pancakes and set two on Emily's plate before putting three on his own. Then he lifted the syrup carafe and held it over Emily's pancakes. "Syrup?"

"Yes, please!"

He poured the syrup. "More?"

"More!"

Jeremy laughed and added another pour.

Kara watched the exchange between her daughter and Jeremy with interest and affection unfurling in her chest. Emily seemed so comfortable with him, and he was really good with her. An ache deep inside squeezed her lungs, making her breathing tight.

Irene brought over a plate piled high with bacon and set it on the table before she took the seat next to Kara. Rick came into the room and took his seat at the table.

When the Hamiltons connected hands and extended open palms toward Kara and Emily, a rush of pleasure threaded through Kara. It had been a long time since she'd sat at a family dinner table.

Even when she was married, she and David had barely had time for a meal together, and when they did connect, it was usually takeout and on the go. Even after Emily was born, their schedules had conflicted. Having moments like this had been nonexistent.

Kara took hold of Irene's hand and then Emily's hand. Jeremy wiggled his fingers to encourage Emily to take his hand.

Emily looked at Kara, her eyes big and questioning.

"You can take his hand," Kara told her. "Then someone will say grace."

Emily slipped her hand into Jeremy's and shouted, "Grace."

Laughing, Kara met Jeremy's eyes over her daughter's head. A shared bond of delight over Emily arced between them. Attraction flared. Her resolve to stay detached wobbled. She forced her gaze away.

"That's the spirit," Rick said. "Now, everyone, close your eyes and bow your head."

Kara peeked from the slit of her half-closed eyes to watch her daughter, who watched all the adults before she closed her eyes and bowed her head. Tender love filled Kara for her little girl along with a sadness at the lack of family in their lives.

"Dear Father in Heaven, bless this food to our bodies and our bodies to your service," Rick said. "Amen."

Kara murmured, "Amen."

Emily leaned over to half whisper, "Why are we praying? It's not bedtime."

Kara's heart twisted with tender affection and a twinge of guilt. "God loves to hear our prayers any time of the day. Not just at bedtime."

Emily seemed to consider this as she straightened. Then as only a child could do, she dug into the pancakes on her plate with gusto.

As soon as they were done with breakfast and the dishes cleared away, Kara had a moment alone with Jeremy while Irene and Rick took Emily down to the water.

"As soon as your parents return with Emily, we can leave," she said.

Jeremy said, "Would you be open to letting Emily stay here with Mom and Dad?"

Before Kara could answer she heard a squeal of delight. She turned to the open front door to find Jeremy's younger sister running toward her with her arms extended.

"Oh, my word," Julia exclaimed. "Tarren said you were here. I didn't think I'd see the day you'd set foot back on our shores."

Kara had half a second before Julia launched herself for a hug. "The best-laid plans."

Julia released Kara and stared into her eyes. "Are you okay? Tarren said there was some trouble at your house. And you have a daughter? Where's your husband? Where's your daughter? Tell me everything."

Kara laughed. Some things never changed. Julia was still the firecracker she'd always been. She'd grown into a beautiful woman. She wore her long strawberry hair in a braid down her back, and her bright eyes were filled with delight.

"Jules, take a breath," Jeremy said with irritation threading through his words.

Interesting. The siblings' dynamics hadn't changed. Kara waved him away. "Don't go all big brother on her. She's fine. We've a lot of catching up to do." To Julia, she said, "I'll be here for at least another night. Maybe we can—"

"Have dinner," Julia supplied, cutting her off. "You can come to my place, or we can go out."

"Yes." Kara laughed. "Dinner would be lovely."

Just then the back sliding door opened. Irene, Rick and Emily stepped inside. Emily ran to Kara and wrapped her arms around her leg and stared up shyly at the newcomer.

Julia squatted down to eye level with Emily. "Hi there. I'm Julia. Who are you?"

"Emily."

Sticking out her hand, Julia said, "Nice to meet you, Emily. I like your Christmas outfit."

Emily stared up at Kara.

"It's all right. Shake her hand."

Emily extended her hand and shook Julia's hand vigorously. "Nice to meet you."

"Do you like turtles?" Julia asked.

Emily nodded eagerly as she wrapped her arms around Kara's leg again.

"Good. I work with turtles. While you're here I'll make sure you get to meet a few."

Emily grinned at Kara. "Mommy, I get to meet turtles."

Kara wasn't sure when that would happen. But she didn't want to dampen the hope in her daughter's eyes. "We'll have to find time."

Julia stood. "I'm not working today. But tomorrow, I'd love for you guys to stop by the Safe Haven Turtle Sanctuary."

Kara tucked in her chin. "I didn't know you were working there."

Of course she didn't. Why would she?

But the career choice was right. Julia had always loved animals and had a generous, protective heart. The turtle sanctuary was the perfect place for her.

It occurred to Kara that in her desire to keep her heart safe from being hurt more by Jeremy, she'd cut all of these good people who she really cared about out, too. Regret churned in her gut.

"What are you guys doing right now?"

"We're headed out to do some errands," Jeremy interjected. He turned to his mother. "Would it be okay if Emily stayed with you?"

"Of course," Irene said. "We can make cookies to take to the church's Christmas bazaar."

Emily clapped her hands. "Cookies."

"Mom, do you mind if I help?" Julia asked.

"The more the merrier," Irene said. She clapped her hands. "Okay, bakers. Let's get baking."

Emily released her hold on Kara's leg and happily skipped into the kitchen with Irene and Julia. Kara wanted to weep with gratitude to the two women for taking such good care of her daughter.

Rick put his hand on Kara's shoulder. "We'll keep her safe."

She hugged him with tears pricking the back of her eyes. "Thank you."

"Shall we?" Jeremy said.

"Let me just grab my creds," she said, referring to her badge and credentials along with her sidearm.

Even though she was technically on vacation, she rarely went anywhere without what she fondly referred to as her armor.

Kara made quick work of pinning her badge to her belt loop, retrieving her Glock 19 from the portable safe she traveled with and tucking her leather-folded credentials into the pocket of her blazer.

She slipped the black semiautomatic pistol into the holster at the low of her back. Making sure the weapon was not visible beneath her jacket, she grabbed her backpack-style purse and hurried out of the house to climb into the passenger seat of Jeremy's police vehicle.

"So what's with Julia and Tarren?" she asked as she buckled in.

It seemed odd to her that Tarren would reveal police information to a civilian. Even if she was the police chief's sister. Not that the information Tarren had revealed was necessarily confidential.

"They're engaged," Jeremy replied.

So not just a civilian. But soon to be a spouse.

The information sank in. Julia and Tarren were an item. Kara had always suspected the two would end up together one day. There had been no mistaking the feelings between Jeremy's best friend and his little sister, even back when they were teens. She also couldn't stop the spurt of envy.

She was happy for them. "Well, it's about time."

Jeremy slanted her glance. "What does that mean?"

"Oh, come on, you had to have known they had feelings for each other."

Jeremy frowned and kept his gaze forward. "No, actually, I didn't. Not until last year, when Julia was targeted by a cartel."

Kara sucked in a breath. "I heard about that nasty business

on the island from Special Agent in Charge Clark. I hadn't realized Julia was the target."

Or that Jeremy was the police chief Clark had raved about. She should have asked more questions, but she'd tamped down her curiosity, unwilling to open old wounds.

Ha. Best laid plans, indeed.

Jeremy glanced in the rearview mirror, then checked the side mirrors. He stepped on the gas. Tension radiated off him in waves.

An answering tension strained her nerves. "Is something wrong?"

The grim set of his jaw didn't bode well. "We have a tail."

The big red truck kept two car lengths between them. Jeremy had noticed it almost immediately when they left his parents' neighborhood after breakfast. Had the truck been lying in wait for them to leave the house? Or was this just a fluke?

Kara twisted in her seat to look through the rear window. "The license plate is obscured with mud."

"I don't recognize the truck," he said as he maneuvered around a mail truck.

She turned back around to face forward. "You have all the vehicles on the island memorized?"

Shooting her a quick glance, he noted her arched eyebrow. "No. Of course not."

"But you feel that you should." Her tone was matter-of-fact. "You've always had a strong sense of responsibility and duty. Which I'm sure this town, this island benefits from."

"Kind of a necessary job requirement." He bypassed Kara's old neighborhood and headed toward town. "We'll see how far this guy follows us."

Jeremy couldn't get a good look at the driver through the review or side-view mirrors because the person had their sunshade down and wore dark sunglasses and a ball cap. The passenger wore the same get-up. The girth of the shoulders of both occupants was massive enough to suggest two males.

"You should radio for backup," she said.

He could tell she was keeping an eye on the truck through the passenger-side mirror.

Not that he could blame her for being on high alert.

After walking in on an intruder last night, not to mention having her house in Virginia ransacked, Kara had to be feeling a bit vulnerable and uneasy.

"There's nothing illegal about us both heading in the same direction," he said.

"True." She rubbed at her temple. "But hard not to be paranoid at the moment."

After what she'd gone through last night, he didn't blame her for the caution. He would do whatever he could to help her through this ordeal. Being targeted for some unknown reason had to be stressful. And concerning as a mother.

Her love for her daughter was obvious. That she was a widow made his heart hurt. He wondered why God had brought her back into his life.

He made the turn onto the main street leading downtown. Behind them, the truck made the same turn.

"Hang on." He took a sharp right, heading for the nearest shopping center entrance.

The truck sped up, gaining on them until its bumper kissed the back end of Jeremy's vehicle.

The SUV fishtailed, the wheel jerking out of Jeremy's hand and putting them on a collision course with an oncoming car.

Was this how they would die?

FOUR

Regripping the wheel, Jeremy turned the SUV at the last second, barely missing the four-door sedan. The driver, a teenager, gaped at them as they passed within inches of each other.

Heart thumping, Jeremy checked the rearview mirror. The truck slowed at the intersection, then raced away and merged into traffic. Jeremy took his foot off the gas as he watched until the truck was out of view.

Kara released her grip on the dashboard. "Good driving. That was close."

"Too close." Jeremy turned the SUV around.

Keeping an eye out for the truck, he steered back onto the main street that ran through town. He radioed dispatch and put an alert out for the red truck. He wanted to bust the driver for his reckless driving.

She let out a noisy breath. "Would you mind if we grabbed a coffee on the way? It may be counterintuitive, but I need something to settle my nerves."

He stopped for a red light. "Sure. I totally understand. I could use a jolt of caffeine myself to release some feel-good dopamine."

A soft smile played on her lips. "I'm glad you get me."

His heart rate ticked up with a yearning to thread their fingers and tug her closer.

Whoa. Where'd that thought come from?

Not smart, dude. She'd dumped you once; she'll do it again.

He swallowed back the truth of the thought and returned his gaze to the road while staying alert for any sign of the red truck.

"Thank you again for what you did last night," she said. "Emily and I both slept well, felt safe."

Music to his ears. He, however, hadn't been able to rest knowing she was so close yet so far away. "I'm glad to hear you were able to rest."

So many questions about her life crammed up his throat, but he held them back. A healthy curiosity was a good thing in law enforcement but not so much when it came to his ex-rival turned girlfriend turned ex-love.

He found a spot right in front of the local coffee shop and parked.

Kara had her door popped open and was out before he'd turned the engine off. She'd never been one to wait around for others. A go-getter. A trait he understood and admired.

Inside the coffee shop, an updated version of "Rockin' Around the Christmas Tree" played. The smells of gingerbread and vanilla saturated the air.

The barista at the counter wore a Santa hat and a string of lights around her neck. She was young and smiled enthusiastically at Kara and Jeremy. "Happy holidays. What merry drink can we get for you today?"

Stepping up to the counter, Kara asked, "Are you still making pumpkin spice lattes?"

"Yes, ma'am," the young woman said. "What size?"

"Make it a large, with an extra shot."

The young woman hit buttons on the computer screen.

"What can I get you, Chief?" The young girl waited with her fingers poised over the screen.

"I'll take a large peppermint-bark latte with an extra shot."

"You got it."

Before Jeremy had a chance to reach for his wallet, Kara was already handing over her credit card.

"You don't—" Jeremy started to say, but Kara held up a hand.

"You're driving me around," she said. "My treat. It's the least I can do."

Knowing better than to argue with the lady, he acknowledged her gift for what it was with a nod. He stepped away from the counter and stood off to the side to lean against the wall where he could watch the door.

Outside the traffic was light, but he knew as the day went on locals and tourists alike would emerge from their dwellings and the town would fill up.

A flash of red caught his attention. Was it the same truck that had tried to make them crash?

He pushed away from the wall. "I'll be outside," he told Kara.

Jeremy didn't want to upset her any more than necessary. He was probably being overly cautious and didn't need to protect her sensibilities, but still, if he could save her some angst, he would. Plus, there was more than one red truck on the island—not to mention the whole state of Texas, for that matter.

He pushed out through the door into the morning sunshine, glancing up and down the festively decorated Main Street of South Padre Island. He searched for any indications of the red truck or the massive men inside. But there was no sign of either.

The coffee-shop door opened behind him, and Kara stepped out, carrying a tray with their drinks. He unlocked the SUV and opened the door for her.

"I grabbed a candy cane." She held up a red-and-white peppermint stick, then tucked it into the pocket of his shirt. "I remember you always liked those."

He grinned, pleased that she remembered. "That I do."

Once they were settled in the SUV, he asked, "So what's the plan?"

Kara sipped from her latte. "Plan?"

He didn't miss the faux not-understanding-what-he-meant tone. She'd always been a planner. "With the house? Are you going to box everything up and ship it to Virginia?"

"Probably not," she said. "I just need to find some documents. Then I plan to have the real estate agent—Joyce Henderson...do you know her?"

"Sure, I know Joyce," he said, thinking of the powerhouse dynamo that was Joyce Henderson. "She's a good choice."

"I'm going to have her donate everything to charity," she said. "If I see something that has sentimental value, I may take it. But I can't imagine that after all this time there's much there that I would want or need."

Putting a voice to one of his burning questions, he ventured, "Why did your mother keep the house?"

"Why indeed?" Kara said. "I really don't know. I asked her that question repeatedly over the years. It seemed like such a waste. But she would always say she had her reasons."

"Maybe she couldn't let go of the memory of your father," Jeremy said. "I've seen that happen with others."

"Maybe. But if that was the case, why did she make us leave?"

Jeremy wondered the same question as he pulled into the driveway of the Evanses' family home.

In the light of day, the house looked like it had when they were young. Mrs. Evans had paid for immaculate upkeep. The small lawn in the front had been mowed, the flowers watered. It had never made sense to him. Was it simply a case of sentimentality?

He guessed they would never know now that she had passed on.

This time, Kara did not hop out of the car immediately but remained in her seat staring at the home where she'd grown up.

"Are you sure you're up for this?" he asked her. "Joyce could go through the house and find whatever it is you need."

"I'm fine. I was just thinking about the intruder, wondering what he was looking for."

"Understandable." But he was with her now. She would be safe. "I've got your back."

She breathed in and let out a long exhale. "This is something I have to do. I need closure. Everything happened so quickly back then."

The pain of her being ripped away from him swelled within his chest. "We barely were given a chance to say goodbye."

She turned to look at him. Her violet-blue eyes searched his face. "There's nothing we can do to change the past. All we can do is move forward and hope that we do better."

With that cryptic remark, she opened the door, hopped out and slung her bag over her shoulders.

Jeremy took a beat to collect his composure. Since she was the one who'd dumped him, he supposed her words made sense to her. After all, she'd moved on and married someone else.

A spurt of hurt erupted, but he tamped it down.

Ancient history.

Lord, I need your peace right now.

Taking his coffee, he climbed out of the vehicle and followed her to the door.

For a moment, déjà vu spun through him. But they weren't teenagers anymore. They weren't in love. Too much time had passed. He was here to help her through the messy business of packing up this part of her life. She said she'd wanted closure.

But there were too many unresolved issues.

Like who was targeting Kara? Who killed her father? Were the two cases linked?

Jeremy didn't know, but he was determined to find out.

Inside the house where she'd grown up, Kara opened all the blinds, letting the December sunlight flood the living room and kitchen. The remnants of the forensic team's dusting for prints remained in the smears of black powder on all available surfaces.

She knew they wouldn't find the intruder's identity. The man had had gloves on. A sense of violation crept through her just as it had earlier in the week when her own house in Virginia had been robbed, making her skin crawl with anger.

Ignoring the living room and kitchen, she headed toward the bedrooms down the hall. Behind her, she heard Jeremy, but it was too much to deal with the emotions he stirred within her on top of the grief and sorrow rising from the depths of her soul. And being in the house where she'd lived with her parents only added to the crushing sensation clogging her throat and hurting her heart.

She missed her father so much. Every day she prayed that God would reveal his killer. But she knew after this much time, the likelihood of his case being solved was close to nil.

She stopped in the doorway of her parents' bedroom as tears pricked her eyes. The room was just as she remembered.

The dark green cover over the bed. Two dressers. One

for her father and one for her mother. The faint scent of Old Spice teased her senses.

Surely it was nothing more than a phantom memory of her father's favorite cologne. She'd always buy him a new bottle at Christmastime.

Squaring her shoulders, she moved deeper into the room. Where would her mother and father have kept those documents?

She quickly looked through the dresser drawers. Her mother's dresser was empty.

However, the sight of her father's neatly folded shirts and socks had her heart contracting painfully in her chest.

On top of the dresser, she ran her hand over the smooth surface of the wooden box that housed his watch collection. He'd always said a man without a watch was a man who didn't value time.

In the closet, his clothes hung untouched. A layer of dust covered the tops of the garments. There were a few boxes sitting on the shelves above her father's clothing. Her mother had taken all of her own clothing with them.

Kara stretched for the closest box but couldn't quite reach it.

"Here, let me," Jeremy said from behind her.

His low masculine tone sent a shiver of attentiveness racing over her flesh. Her breath hitched. She hadn't heard him enter the room. For a moment, she wanted nothing more than to step into his embrace.

With effort, she reined in her reaction and stepped out of the way with a gesture for him to go ahead.

The heat of his big, muscled chest enveloped her as he moved past and easily retrieved the first box. He offered it to her.

Their hands brushed.

Sensation skittered up her arm.

She snatched the box and moved quickly to set it on the bed.

He brought the second box over. "Do you want to just take these with us?"

"I should at least glance through them and make sure they have what I need." Though she made no move to open the lids.

"There are more boxes in your father's study," he said.

She lifted her gaze to him. "Gone exploring already?"

The gold in his eyes darkened. "I wanted to give you a moment."

Always the gentleman. Even when they were preteens, he'd been so courteous and thoughtful. All the girls in school had had a crush on him. It had taken her a while to come to the same conclusion as her peers.

Jeremy Hamilton was a catch.

And for a short time, he'd been hers.

Until he hadn't.

"Why aren't you married?" The question popped out unbidden.

Immediately, regret and embarrassment infused her chest with heat that crept up her neck and into her cheeks. She wasn't usually so forward when it came to personal matters.

But this was Jeremy.

And having him here distracted her from the grief that was so close to the surface that she was afraid at any moment she might break down.

He arched a brown eyebrow. "I suppose I've been too focused on my career. Doesn't leave a lot of time for anything else."

"I understand," she said. Her fingers toyed with the lid of the first box. "David and I were both very dedicated to our jobs. He had his sights set on director. He'd always been ambitious. It was one of the things that drew me to him. We pushed each other to excel."

She peered up at Jeremy, her gaze tracing the angles and planes of his cheekbones, jaw and lips. His face was so familiar, yet they were strangers. "Kind of like you and me when we were kids. I wanted to beat you so badly. But I never could."

His grin was devastating.

Her knees wobbled.

"You were better than most of the guys on the team. That's one of the reasons they resented you." He seemed to sober. "You're right, though—we did push each other. I knew you were in competition with me for your father's attention."

"I was pathetic." She turned away and ripped the lid off the first box. Inside were stacks of loose photos.

Jeremy's hand took hold of her elbow, his touch warm and gentle enough to make her want to lean into him.

"Never pathetic." His tone was soft, soothing. "You were fierce. Dedicated and determined. Traits that make you a very good FBI agent. A good profiler."

She pulled in a shaky breath. She shouldn't like his compliment so much. "Thank you for saying that."

"Hey." He turned her to face him. "I'm not paying you lip service. It's true. I've kept up on your career. You've done amazing things. Your father would be very proud of you."

The tears she'd been holding back finally crested and ripped down her cheeks. "He would've been proud of you as well."

Jeremy's lips twisted. "Fat lot of good my becoming police chief has done for him. You know, I still look at his case file every few months, trying to find something that will help me discover who killed him and why."

"I did the same for years after I joined the Bureau," she

admitted. "One of the first things I did was request a copy from the then–police chief."

"I know," Jeremy said. "He told me when he retired."

She wasn't surprised. The beloved high school baseball coach's murder had rocked the island. "But my therapist helped me to see obsessing over the past was keeping me from enjoying the present."

"You certainly have a reason to enjoy your life now," Jeremy said as he stepped back, putting space between them. "Emily is adorable."

For some reason, she sensed he was emotionally withdrawing, but she wasn't sure she wanted to dig too deeply into his reason why. "She took to you and your family quicker than I've seen her do with anyone else."

She replaced the lid on the box of photos and moved to the second box. Inside were trinkets that she'd never seen before.

A Russian nesting doll in bold reds, yellows and oranges. A box full of old coins from different countries.

Baseball cards were rubber-banded together. "These must've been my father's. I'll take these two boxes with me."

"There's room in both boxes for more items," Jeremy murmured softly.

She glanced around the room, ready to let go of the past. "Let's check out my dad's office."

A thorough search of the desk, closet and bookshelf revealed nothing of importance. The boxes were old taxes and school records, which could all be shredded and recycled.

"If not the office or their bedroom," Kara said, "then where would they have stored important papers?"

"Are you sure your mother didn't take the documents with her?"

"When I asked her about her will, life insurance policies and the mortgage papers, Mom said everything I needed is here." She shrugged. "When I asked why she didn't bring them with us, she grew agitated and said my father always handled stuff like that."

He tilted his head. "Would she have stored them in your old bedroom?"

Kara made a face at the idea. "Doubtful. But I guess we can check."

Walking into her old bedroom was like stepping back in time. The room was painted a bright chartreuse green and *Peanuts* characters decorated the bedding. She'd been big into Snoopy and Woodstock.

It was exactly as she left it that day twelve years ago when she and her mother had jumped into her uncle's car and he'd driven them to Corpus Christi. They had flown to Virginia, where her mother and uncle had grown up.

Kara's yearbooks were stacked on a shelf above the small desk. A layer of dust covered everything. She checked the drawers of the desk and under the bed, then the empty closet.

Though she found several items that she wanted to take for Emily, like her baton and leather baseball mitt, there were no important documents to be found.

"Maybe they're with my uncle." Thinking of her uncle Don, she grimaced. She'd been remiss in not letting him know she was in town. "But why would my mom tell me to come here? And if my uncle had everything, then why wouldn't he have told me?"

"When was the last time you saw your uncle?"

"He came to visit my mother a month before she passed," she said. "He comes a few times a year to visit. That's how I learned you had joined the police force."

She remembered adamantly telling her uncle she wanted no more information about Jeremy Hamilton. They never spoke of Jeremy again.

"Maybe you should call and ask him?"

"I will." She adjusted the strap of her backpack to a more comfortable position on her shoulder. "There's a couple more places we can check. The garage, for one." She pointed upward. "And there's a small attic space."

In the hallway ceiling, they found the pull-down lever for the ladder that led to the crawlspace above the bedrooms. They made quick work of dropping the ladder and climbing up.

The attic space was filled with dust motes dancing in the sunlight coming through the small round window at the apex of the house. There were more boxes to go through.

As they moved, the floorboards creaked with disuse and age.

Jeremy pulled a plaid blanket off a lump under the window to reveal an old wooden chest.

"How did that get up here?" The old chest had been her mother's hope chest, and at one time, her mother had said it would be hers.

But it had been left behind.

"It used to sit in my parents' bedroom." She hadn't noticed it missing earlier.

Out of sight, out of mind, she supposed.

"This is a beautiful piece." Jeremy ran a hand over the intricately carved wood depicting a woodland scene with deer and other forest creatures among swaying trees and flowers.

"It was my mother's," Kara told him. "Her grandfather brought it over from Europe after World War Two." There was a lock on the latch. "I don't have the key for that."

"We can break it, if that's okay?" Jeremy said.

"Have at it," Kara told him.

He removed the hefty utility flashlight from his duty belt. It took two good whacks before the lock mechanism gave way. He removed the lock and scooted back so she could open the lid.

Inside, she found several quilts that dated back to her great-grandmother. She pulled each item out and smoothed a hand over the material. These she'd keep for Emily.

More photos lined a tray at the bottom of the chest. These were photographs of her mother's family in Virginia. More keepsakes.

Carefully, Kara and Jeremy lifted the tray out of the chest. Empty. Frustration tightened her shoulder muscles. Where were the documents she needed?

Jeremy stared at the chest for a moment, then began tapping at the bottom. "This has a false bottom."

He reached inside and felt around. A click of a small lever echoed through the attic. The bottom popped up enough for her and Jeremy to lift it out of the chest.

Kara stared down into the belly of the chest. A gasp escaped her.

Wrapped in plastic was a baseball bat covered in dried blood.

The weapon used to murder her father?

FIVE

Kara's gasp echoed through the attic space. Standing next to her, it took a moment for Jeremy to process what he was seeing at the bottom of the elaborately carved wooden chest.

"Is that…?"

"My missing baseball bat." Kara lifted her shocked gaze to meet his. "Was my bat used to kill my father?"

The color drained from her face.

Nervous she'd come unglued, Jeremy put his hands on her shoulders. "We don't know anything yet. Let's not assume."

Her body shook beneath his hands. "Not assume? All I have are assumptions and theories. Did my mother…?"

She jerked away from him and paced the length of the attic space. "No, no, no. This can't be happening."

Jeremy's gut twisted with dread. Could this be the murder weapon that was used to kill Coach Evans?

Why was it in this hope chest?

Had Laine Evans been involved in her husband's brutal murder?

Kara stopped pacing and stood with her fists clenched. "Is this why my mother wouldn't sell the house? Did she put that there?"

Jeremy's heart clenched. "You can't think your mother used the bat against your father."

"And why not? What other explanation could there be? Who else would have had access?"

Running a hand through his hair, Jeremy fought for a calm that was proving elusive. "You know the facts of the case as well as I do. Whoever bludgeoned your father used great force. Do you honestly believe your mother had that much physical power?"

Kara seemed to deflate. "No. She didn't."

She chopped the air with a hand as if chopping through his argument. "But she could've had an accomplice."

A hard glint shone in her pretty eyes, replacing the shock. "The same person who broke into my house in Virginia and who I interrupted last night could have been her partner in crime. The intruder was looking for the bat."

A hypothesis that Jeremy agreed with but that also raised questions. "If that were true, then why didn't her accomplice already know where the bat was? And why wait all these years?"

"We need to find the intruder and ask him."

Not as easy as it sounded.

He gestured to the bat. "We need to get this to the forensics lab. Confirm that it's your father's blood on the bat. See if we can lift prints."

A visible shudder ran over Kara. "Can we go now? We can come back later to keep looking for the documents."

"Yes." Jeremy grabbed another quilt to wrap around the plastic-encased bat and lifted it from the bottom of the hope chest. Then he recovered the chest with the plaid quilt. "I'll have our forensic team come dust the chest for prints."

The tinkling of shattering glass echoed through the quiet house.

"Someone's breaking in," Kara half whispered.

She quickly pulled up the retractable ladder and shut the hatch to the attic. "They can't know we found it."

Carefully placing the quilt-enshrouded evidence on top of the hope chest, Jeremy held up a hand, indicating for her not to move.

If either of them stepped on a creaking board, it would alert the intruder to their presence. However, whoever was breaking in had to have seen his vehicle in the driveway.

Had they peered through the windows and decided no one was inside?

He hoped they hadn't seen the retractable ladder.

They heard male voices, but the words were indistinguishable.

At least two men were searching the house. Presumably, one was the same person that Kara had interrupted the night before, but this time, he'd brought a friend. The two men from the red truck?

They had to be looking for the bat.

Jeremy itched to apprehend the suspects but climbing down from the attic would put them in a precarious and vulnerable position. He wouldn't do anything that put Kara in jeopardy.

After standing still for ten minutes, Jeremy's legs began to shake from the inactivity. He met Kara's gaze. She gave him a look, communicating that she, too, was becoming fatigued from standing in place for so long.

Another ten minutes later, when there was no more noise in the house, Jeremy chanced to shift his weight. The floorboard beneath him creaked. His breath stalled in his chest.

For a long tense moment, he waited in anticipation of someone opening the hatch and lowering the ladder. His muscles bunched and his hand rested on his sidearm.

Another few minutes ticked by without being discovered.

Kara was the first to relax. She staggered to sit on a box. "I think they're gone."

Jeremy prayed so. But he couldn't risk someone getting their hands on the evidence that might finally put to rest the cold case of Coach Evans's murder and bring the killer to justice.

He picked up the wrapped bat and followed Kara down the retractable ladder. She had her weapon drawn and held at the ready.

"Obviously they didn't find what they were looking for," Kara said as they peeked into the bedrooms that were now torn apart.

Maybe the intruder had come to finish the job from the night before.

Carrying the bat, Jeremy moved through the house and found the point of entry in the kitchen. The window over the sink had been broken. A muddy shoe print marred the counter where the intruders had climbed in. The back slider stood open where they had left.

"I'm calling this in." He reported the break-in and had the forensic team once again dispatched to the house. When he finished with the call, he said, "I still think we need to do a thorough search. There are boxes in the garage that need to be gone through. And you haven't found the documents you need."

"I agree. Whoever broke in thankfully didn't know about the attic space."

"But we'll have to come back." Jeremy hustled Kara out of the house into his vehicle. He placed the bat on the floor at her feet.

The sensation of being watched tripped down his spine. Before he climbed in, he glanced around the quiet neighborhood, looking for a place where somebody might be hiding.

They could be anywhere, from a neighbor's yard to one of the civilian cars parked along the street. He didn't see the big red truck, but that didn't mean it wasn't close by.

To be on the safe side, he took surface streets through the neighborhoods. Much easier to determine if they were being followed. So far they were good.

When he came to the fork in the road where he had to turn left to go to the beach or right to go downtown, the big red truck roared down the street behind them, heading straight for them.

Needing to keep civilians safe, Jeremy cranked the wheel to the left and headed toward the beach. The truck rounded the corner on squealing tires before charging forward.

Jeremy stepped on the gas.

Kara banged her fist on the dashboard. "Where were they?"

With no time to answer, Jeremy had another decision to make: Turn into the beach parking lot, or take his vehicle out onto the sand?

Again, mindful of civilians, he jumped the small barrier separating the pavement from the beach. His SUV went airborne for a moment before it landed with a painful thudding impact on the dry sand.

In the rearview mirror, he watched the truck racing to follow.

"Move!" Kara yelled.

Jeremy gritted his teeth, eased up on the gas and turned the wheel so that the vehicle spun. The back end barely moved out of the way before the red truck hit the sand.

"Call for backup," he ground out. He didn't dare take his hands off the wheel to use his radio.

Kara shrugged off her backpack and grabbed her cell phone from a pocket.

Jeremy switched on the four-wheel-drive hydraulics and barreled down the sand with lights and sirens blaring. All around them were tourists and beachcombers. Someone was going to get hurt. He honked for added encouragement for people to move out of the way.

He pulled the crank on the emergency brake, sending the vehicle into a slide as he spun the wheel so that he faced the oncoming truck.

"Are you kidding me?" Kara said as she hit 911. "You're playing chicken?"

"Better to play offense than defense."

"Just don't kill us."

Kara talked into her phone, telling the dispatcher they needed help.

Her voice sounded much calmer than Jeremy felt.

"Hang on." He veered off course of the oncoming truck and steered the SUV for the wet sand where the tires would get more purchase. He sent up a silent prayer of gratitude that it wasn't turtle-nesting season.

Barely missing the truck that was still heading in the opposite direction, he drove along the shore toward North Padre Island National Seashore State Park.

The big red truck did a U-turn in a spray of sand and chased after them.

When they reached the Mansfield Cut, the artificial waterway bisecting the island, Jeremy's heart sank. There was nowhere for him to go. The big truck bore down on them. He didn't have time to turn the SUV around.

The truck was going to ram them.

"Brace yourself." He could only hope that whoever was driving would become incapacitated by the impact of the truck crashing into the SUV.

The red truck made contact, the front grill crushing the

back compartment of the police SUV. The deafening noise of the two vehicles colliding shuddered through him. He was jolted into the steering wheel.

The airbag deployed with force, pushing him back against the seat. Kara's airbag also deployed. The cab of the SUV was filled with white powder as the cushions puffed up, then quickly deflated.

The sound of screeching metal bending and twisting rang in Jeremy's ears as he stomped on the brake, trying to prevent the truck from pushing them into the ocean.

But the bigger truck had more power. Bigger tires. And despite how heavy Jeremy's foot was on the brake, the SUV plowed into the salty water.

"We have to save the bat!" Kara yelled.

She fought the white airbag to reach down at her feet to grab the quilt-wrapped bat. She lifted the evidence over her head. The interior of the SUV filled with water coming up through the floorboards.

A shadow appeared next to Kara's window.

Alarmed, Jeremy jerked against the seat belt, but it held him in place.

The assailant wore a ski mask and used a handheld device to shatter the passenger-side window. He reached in to grab the evidence from Kara.

Frustration revved through Jeremy's veins. He'd been right. Someone had watched them leave Kara's home.

She held on. "No. Let go!"

Jeremy pressed the release button on his seat belt, but the mechanism wouldn't unbuckle. He yanked at the strap, unsuccessfully trying to climb out of the restraint so he could help Kara.

He could slide his weapon from his holster, but there was

no way he could fire at the man without risking Kara's safety. He reached for the knife on his utility belt.

The man trying to wrest the bat from her reared back and punched Kara in the face.

Her head snapped back and the bat was ripped from her hands.

Clearly dazed, Kara moaned. Her eyes closed and she slumped in the seat.

"No!" Jeremy quickly sawed through the seat belt. He had to help Kara.

Another masked man appeared beside the first one.

"Boss wants her, too," the first man yelled, his voice harsh and raspy. He turned and waded away toward the red truck with the evidence held high out of the water's reach.

The second man reached inside and grasped ahold of Kara by the shoulders, trying to drag her out the shattered window, but the seat belt held her in place.

Jeremy scrambled from his seat and reached across Kara to shove his gun into the masked man's face.

The man released his hold on her and splashed away.

The two men jumped into the truck and took off in a spray of sand and ocean water.

And with them, the evidence Jeremy and Kara needed to close her father's cold murder case.

"That's going to leave a nasty bruise." Julia held Kara's hand and inspected her face.

Embarrassed that she had been clocked by the assailant and involuntarily lost her grip enough on the bat long enough for it to be wrenched away from her, Kara seethed silently. Her face ached where the jerk's fist had connected with her cheekbone.

The sounds and smells of the hospital normally bothered

Kara, reminding her too much of loss, but now, as she sat in a chair of the emergency department, she barely noticed.

Her gaze strayed to Jeremy, standing a few feet away, dripping wet as he and Tarren discussed what happened. It was all a bit of a blur.

She remembered taking the hit to the face. The cool water rapidly filled the SUV and enveloped her up to her biceps. Then Jeremy and Tarren pulled her out of the vehicle and onto the dry sand, where paramedics fussed over her until they put her on a litter and carried her to the ambulance bay.

She'd closed her eyes on the ride to the hospital, breathing through the throbbing pain radiating through her face.

At the hospital, she'd been rushed inside to see a doctor who said she'd have some bruising and a headache, but thankfully, she didn't have a concussion. Now she waited to be released.

"If I'd had my hands free," Kara said between clenched teeth, "this wouldn't have happened."

"From what I understand," Julia said, "the SUV plunged into window-high water. There wasn't a lot you could do in that situation."

Kara hated having lost the evidence that could have finally solved her father's murder. And the bad guys would probably destroy it. She'd never have the closure she and Jeremy sought. At least now she knew the break-ins were connected with the cold case.

With a sigh of resignation, Kara tilted her head at Julia. "How did you know to come to the hospital?"

"Tarren called on his way back from the scene," Julia informed her. "He made sure a tow truck got Jeremy's SUV out of the ocean."

Remorse for how Jeremy's vehicle had faired slithered through Kara. He was going to be without his own wheels for the foreseeable future. At least the police station probably had another vehicle available to him.

She placed her hands on her head and massaged her temples. Her head throbbed and she wasn't thinking clearly.

She heard the squish of Jeremy's steps as he hustled to her side. He crouched down in front of her and put his hands on her knees. "Has the doctor looked at you?"

"Yes," she said. "He agreed with the paramedics. No concussion. Just a bruise. I'm going to have a headache for a while."

It occurred to her that whoever assaulted her had pulled the punch at the last second as if he hadn't wanted to do any permanent damage. Why?

It didn't make any sense. Or maybe she wasn't making sense.

Maybe that was as hard as the suspect could hit. A guy who thought hiding behind a mask and decking a woman was cool. Manly.

Her fingers dug into her hair as a fresh wave of anger washed through her.

Oh, she would like nothing better than to show that good-for-nothing what a woman could do.

"Hey." Jeremy's voice pulled her from her thoughts. "The doc says you're good to go. Let's get out of here. There's nothing more that we can do right now. Julia will take you back to my parents'."

She did want to see Emily. And lie down with an ice pack. "I need to call my uncle." She groaned. "My cell phone is unusable. I dropped it in your SUV. It's most likely waterlogged and might even have floated out to sea."

A hint of a smile graced Jeremy's lips. "We can get you a new phone easily enough. Tarren and I will stop at the electronics store."

Kara hated having others do things for her. Relying on others made her feel weak. "I can go."

Jeremy helped her to her feet. "The best thing right now is for you to go see your daughter. And lie down."

She opened her mouth to protest, but he held up a hand, forcing her to hit pause on her words.

"I get it," he said, with just enough self-effacing in his tone to make her arch an eyebrow. "You're strong. Capable. You can fend for yourself. I know. But sometimes, Kara, we need to let others do things for us."

She narrowed her gaze. "When was the last time you let someone do something for you?"

His gaze slid to Julia and then back. "That's a tale for another time."

Kara's gaze jumped to Julia. "Okay."

She winked. "I'll tell you all about it."

Jeremy rolled his eyes at his sister. "Seems your friendship has picked up where it left off. Ganging up on me like the good old days."

Kara couldn't contain the chuckle that rose up from the depths of her heart. Boy, she'd missed these two. "You know it, slugger."

She winced at the nickname she used to call Jeremy. That moniker now had another connotation to it.

Someone had used her bat to kill her father and hidden the evidence in her family home.

She prayed with all her might that her mother wasn't involved, but what else could she think?

"I'll go start the van," Julia said and hustled away.

Kara's head began to pound even more. Her knees wobbled and she swayed.

Jeremy grasped her, pulling her close to his side. "Come on. I'll walk you out."

She should have pushed away and left on her own, but it felt so good to be held against his side, his arm encircling her like they used to do when they were teens. She'd always fancied it was him claiming her as his. But this was not that.

This was him being a gentleman.

Chivalry was not dead.

Kara spotted the Safe Haven Turtle Sanctuary mobile the moment they stepped out of the sliding glass doors of the hospital. The colorfully decorated van sat at an angle, barely inside the two white lines of the parking spot.

Jeremy helped Kara into the passenger seat, and when she went to reach for the buckle he beat her to it. Carefully, he pulled the strap over her, mindful of where the seat belt had slammed across her torso when they'd hit the water.

She hadn't wanted to admit she was sore where the strap had dug into her flesh. Or that her forearms, which had come up the second before the airbags deployed, stung.

She guessed that Jeremy was feeling the same pain. "Were you checked out by the ER doctor?"

"The paramedics," he said. "I didn't sustain an injury to the head. Now, go be with your daughter." He gestured to a police cruiser nearby. "You'll have an escort home. I'll check in with you soon. And I'll bring you a new phone so that you can call your uncle."

She nodded, but when he stepped back to shut the door she couldn't stop herself from reaching out and grabbing a hold of his sleeve. "This wasn't your fault. We knew there was a chance they were following us."

"I didn't see them," he said, self-loathing vibrating in his voice.

"There are many ways to track someone," she said. "They could be high-tech enough to have tracked our phones. Or they could have put a tracker on your SUV."

His gaze hardened. "I'm going to dump my phone as well. We'll both get new phones. And I'll make sure our forensic tech goes over the SUV with a fine-tooth comb. If we do find a tracking device, maybe we can reverse engineer it to help us find the people who did this."

Knowing she was going out on a limb, Kara said, "The FBI has some of the best tech available. Let me know how I can help. I've enough people who owe me favors. Plus, people like me."

His grin flashed. "I have no doubt people like you, Kara. I—" He clamped his lips together in a firm line. He stepped back and shut the door without another word.

"Woo-hoo," Julia said in a singsong voice. "Someone was about to say they like you, too."

Turning to the woman whom she'd once thought would be her sister, Kara arched an eyebrow. "Don't get any ideas about playing matchmaker. Jeremy and I know the score. The past has to stay in the past."

"Yeah, we'll see," Julia said as she started the engine and headed them away from the hospital. "Let me tell you how Tarren and I stopped a cartel that was kidnapping young girls and selling them on the black market. And how Jeremy had to rely on Tarren to protect me." She gave a shudder. "And there was an alligator situation."

All thoughts of Jeremy fled as Kara listened to the harrowing tale that thrust Julia and Tarren together, making them acknowledge their childhood crushes had turned into love.

As happy as Kara was for them, she was sure searching for her father's killer was not going to end so well for her and Jeremy. Someone had used force to obtain the bat. Which meant her father's killer was still at large.

But why try to kidnap her when they stole the evidence? What more did they want?

SIX

The next morning, dressed in a fresh two-piece navy suit and white blouse, Kara put her hair back in a clip and applied concealer over the bruises on her face where the miscreant had punched her the day before.

She seethed at having lost the potential evidence that could finally identify her father's murderer and put the person behind bars. The frustration had kept her from sleeping well.

Julia's words at the hospital came back to taunt Kara. Yes, she and Jeremy had been submerged in water. Yes, the airbags had deployed and the seat-belt mechanism had been damaged, preventing them from stopping the loss of the bat.

Still, she should have been stronger. She should've withstood the punch to the face without losing her grip on the bat.

Tugging on the hem of her suit jacket, she took a deep breath to calm the anxiety clawing up her spine.

Her deceased husband's voice echoed in her head. *You aren't a superhero. It's okay to ask for help.*

Hadn't Jeremy said something similar?

"That may be," she whispered. David had always been so good at knowing what she needed to hear. But he wasn't here.

And Jeremy...she didn't want to go there.

Asking for help didn't come easily to her, but to ensure her safety for Emily's sake, she'd do anything.

She left the guest bedroom that she and Emily shared. Her daughter had already left the room, eager to see the Hamiltons.

After arriving at Jeremy's parents' house last night, Kara had iced her face and watched a movie with Emily about a world of snow and two sisters navigating their complicated relationship with the help of trolls, a funny reindeer and a talking snowman.

Normally, Kara would have sung along with her daughter, but last night the words were a little too poignant. Maybe she needed to let go of her need for closure over her father's murder. Yet, the threat was no longer something in the past but very much in the present. Both of her houses had been burglarized, they'd been run off the road and a man had tried to take her from the truck. For the first time in a long time, closure and revelation seemed possible.

She lifted a prayer that God would lead her and Jeremy to her father's killer. She had to trust that whoever killed her father would be brought to justice.

Her thoughts tumbled back to her mother. Had she been involved?

Had she been so unhappy with her husband that she would resort to ending his life?

Who was her accomplice?

Had Laine Evans's grief all those years ago been manufactured?

A deep ache spread through Kara.

Pausing before entering the kitchen, where Emily sat on a counter barstool and Irene and Rick were preparing breakfast, she closed her eyes and thought back to when she and her mother had heard the news.

Her mother had been hysterical. But a day later, she had gone quiet.

Then she'd announce they were moving to Virginia, where Laine was from.

Kara couldn't say for sure that her mother's grief had been real or not. She'd been so bogged down by her own sorrow to have paid much attention to her mom.

And it hurt too much to think about that day and the days that followed.

The door to the living room opened. Jeremy stepped inside, and all the air in Kara's lungs evaporated. Her heart gave an unexpected bump. Uh-oh.

She quickly reined in her wayward reaction. The last thing she needed was to allow her heart to become tangled up in Jeremy again.

Squaring her shoulders and lifting her chin, she plastered on a smile and said, "Good morning, Jeremy."

His green-gold gaze narrowed. "How are you feeling?"

Her face still throbbed. The bruises across her abdomen and chest were tender. Every movement of her clothing aggravated the discolored skin. But there was no way she would ever admit to any weakness.

She'd fought her whole life to be viewed as competent and equal. "Better. Thank you for asking."

"Mommy!"

Turning, she braced her feet apart as Emily hurled herself into her arms. Pain ricocheted through her body, but Kara gritted her teeth and buried her face into her daughter's soft hair, breathing in deep the wonderful smell of her apple-scented shampoo.

"I'm glad you both are up," Irene said. "Breakfast is just about ready. I would imagine you're famished. Neither of you ate much of your dinner last night."

Setting her daughter on her feet and gingerly straightening, Kara did her best to hide a wince. She appreciated

Irene's mothering, but she could see herself getting a bit overwhelmed if this continued much longer.

She wasn't used to being taken care of. Her mother hadn't been the nurturing type. Kara had loved her but had accepted her for who she was.

And ever since David's death, it had been Kara and Emily. Kara relied heavily on a trusted sitter when she couldn't be with her daughter.

Kara and Jeremy joined the Hamiltons and Emily at the kitchen table. They were about to say grace when Julia and Tarren walked through the living room door.

Behind them, the beautiful dark-colored shepherd trotted in and sniffed the Christmas tree before he made himself at home on the rug in front of the hearth.

"Oh, we're just in time," Julia said as she and Tarren took seats at the table.

Rick's mouth quirked. "You seem to always arrive just as we're sitting down to eat. And having to leave just as we're cleaning up."

Julia grinned. "I love you, too, Dad."

Rick's deep chuckle brought a pang of sorrow to Kara. She missed being a part of a family.

She busied herself doctoring her bowl of oatmeal with real maple syrup and raisins. And she sprinkled a little cinnamon sugar onto Emily's oatmeal.

"Kara, would you mind if I take Emily with me to the sanctuary today?" Julia asked. "Mom gave me a box of extra ornaments to decorate the lobby with, and I could use some help. Plus I can show Emily all the turtles."

"Can I, Mom? Can I?" Emily bounced in her seat.

Kara felt a nudge at her knee. Her gaze jumped to Jeremy.

"That would be a good idea." He nodded encouragingly. "We still have boxes to go through."

Appreciating his thoughtfulness and his sensitivity not to say it would be better if her daughter wasn't underfoot while they finished searching her childhood home, Kara smiled. "Right. I think it's a brilliant idea. I wonder who came up with it?"

Jeremy's gaze dropped to his oatmeal, and he shoved a spoonful into his mouth.

Kara turned her gaze to Tarren. He mimicked Jeremy.

She shook her head. She had no doubt the two had come up with the idea.

Contrary to what Rick had said, she was happy to see Julia stay and help clean up, while Kara and Jeremy set up the new phones he had purchased.

Thankfully all of her contact names and numbers had been uploaded to her cloud storage. She was able to access them online using the Hamiltons' computer.

Snagging the few numbers that were essential for now, she also included Uncle Don's. She still needed to let him know she was in town. Though why she was hesitating, she couldn't say.

It wasn't that she didn't want to see her mother's brother. It was more that she was afraid their shared grief over her mother's passing would be devastating.

But she knew she had to reach out to him.

Once Julia and Emily were off to the turtle sanctuary, Jeremy took Kara back to her childhood home in his personal vehicle, a small SUV. Tarren and Raz followed behind. They were taking no chances this time.

While Tarren and his partner kept watch outside, Kara and Jeremy headed inside. An hour into their search of the garage filled with shelves of boxes and pallets hanging from the ceiling, they came across an old laptop.

"That was my father's." Kara touched the large square piece of electronic equipment.

On the cover, her father had placed a sticker with the high school's logo. Her father had loved being a teacher and coach.

"Let's see if it'll fire up," Jeremy said.

The thing was dead. They looked for a charger but found nothing. Nor did they find the documents Kara was searching for.

"Maybe they're in a safe-deposit box." Kara didn't relish the idea of going to every bank on the island and asking if her mother had kept a safe-deposit box there. But she would if she needed to.

"That's certainly a possibility." Jeremy tucked the large laptop under his arm. "Let's take this back to the station house. I'm sure the head of the forensic team can figure out how to get it charged and accessible. Also, I'll ask one of the deputies to conduct the search for a safe-deposit box. The banks will be more cooperative if the inquiry comes from an official source."

Kara arched an eyebrow. "You don't think the FBI is an official source?"

Jeremy huffed out a sigh. "That's not what I meant. You're a relative. The request might be met with resistance. They may require a court order or an affidavit saying you're the sole heir. Do you have a copy of her death certificate?"

"I do." What he said was true. "I appreciate the assist. Maybe we'll even find a clue to the identity of my father's murderer. Or at least something to lead us to the person who stole the bat. The person who was maybe in league with my mother."

She still couldn't wrap her mind around the idea that her mother was in on her father's murder, but what else was she to think?

Jeremy stared at her. "Does that mean you're planning on staying longer than you'd intended?"

As painful as the memories were of this house, this town and this island, her desire to find her father's murderer was stronger. "My bereavement leave is nearly up, but I've vacation days I could use. I need to check in with my boss, though, and give him an update. I'll see what resources can be allocated to helping us find my father's killer."

Jeremy's face remained impassive. He gave a nod and then headed for the door.

On the sidewalk, they met up with Tarren and Raz.

"We walked the perimeter," Tarren said. "Raz didn't alert."

Jeremy held up the laptop. "We're taking this to the station to see what Vivian can do with it."

"We'll follow you," Tarren said.

The drive to downtown was quick. Once they were inside the brick building of the sheriff's department, Kara allowed herself to be curious about this place that Jeremy ran. Was he a good boss? How had he come to be a police officer, let alone the chief?

As they walked through the neat and orderly department, people seemed to be genuinely friendly to their boss as he passed. That answered one question.

They met with the forensic tech, Vivian Hart, an African American woman in her forties. A white coat covered her clothes, but the edges of a floral shirt peeked out at her collar. She promised to do all that she could to bring power to the laptop. "Hopefully, it's not encrypted. By the way, we found a small tracking device under the rear wheel well on your SUV. I've been unable to trace its signal. It was too damaged."

"Figures," Kara said.

Vivian walked away, taking the laptop with her.

Jeremy rounded his desk, picking up a stack of notes. He shifted through them, sorting them on his desk.

Kara's gaze was riveted to a whiteboard in the corner. The side facing out was blank. But she could see the edge of a photo hanging off the backside. Jeremy had an investigation board.

Old school. She liked it. As a profiler for the FBI, she used a variety of methods to track clues and suspects as well as keep the victim at the forefront. Most were online.

"I have to make a couple of calls." Jeremy sat at his desk.

"Don't mind me." Kara waved her hand at him as she headed for the board.

Awareness tripped down her spine. He was watching her.

He hung up the phone abruptly. "That's an active investigation. I'd prefer you didn't."

Her hand stilled on the board, ready to spin the wheels so that it faced outward.

"Jeremy, I am sure you're unused to having help beyond Tarren and your team here," she said in a modulated tone.

Her heart beat rapidly in her chest, but she did everything she could to keep the flutter of anticipation from showing. "You know what I do. I'm here. Let me help."

Ironic how much easier it was to offer help than it was to accept it. She waited, watching the expression on his face.

One corner of his mouth pulled down.

A facial gesture she remembered when he was deep in thought. He would do that as he stood on the pitcher's mound, deciding which type of spin to put on the ball.

For a long moment, indecision warred in his eyes. He had such beautiful eyes. How many times had she lost herself in his gaze?

Giving herself a mental shake, she reminded herself that

she wasn't going down that road again. But she still held his gaze, waiting.

Slowly, he gave a nod, acquiescing to her request. She spun the whiteboard so that she could see the side filled with photos and Post-it notes in Jeremy's scrawling script and others. She stepped back to get the whole picture.

Photos of three men in rigor mortis were taped across the top of the board. Her breath caught in her throat. "You're not just investigating one murder but multiple on South Padre Island."

Jeremy gritted his teeth and rose from his desk chair. Keeping his gaze on Kara, he strode across his office to shut the door and close the blinds. There were civilians in the building, and the police were trying to keep this quiet. "The last thing we need is the public becoming aware."

Kara dipped her chin and stared at him with her pretty eyes. "Seriously. You think something like this can be kept under wraps for long?"

"No," he confessed. His gut churned with acid. "But every one of my officers is sworn to a code of silence until we have something to reassure the public with. I have an experienced homicide detective working the case."

Kara turned her gaze back to the board. He studied her profile. He'd always liked the straight line of her nose. The perfect bow of her lips. The tiny cleft in her chin. How many times had he placed kisses there, hoping to convince her the little spot she considered an imperfection was actually adorable?

Jerking his gaze away from her, he ran a hand through his hair and looked at the board. *Keep your mind away from the past.*

"The first body was found five days ago." He gestured

to the man they had finally identified. "Levi Marcon. He's originally from Colorado but has been on the island for the past two years."

He moved to the next photo. "Then, a day later, Robbie Carson was found. Also a transplant, from Arizona."

He tapped the third photo. "The last victim, Benny Basher from Brownsville, was discovered the night you arrived."

"Walk me through what you have so far."

For the next hour, Jeremy shared with her what they knew and the evidence they had gathered. Kara asked great questions and had him viewing the situation a bit differently. Did the fact that all three men were not local factor into their murders?

He was impressed with her agile mind.

She had always been a force to be reckoned with on and off the baseball field. She was super smart, way beyond what anyone gave her credit for.

He was glad that she was using her intelligence for good. And if she could help him solve these murders and maybe bring closure to her father's case, all the better. This island was his to protect.

There was a knock at the door, and Vivian stepped inside. "I found the right charger. It'll take a while for that old dinosaur to power up. As soon as it's ready, I'll let you know."

"I appreciate it," he said.

Vivian smiled before retreating, closing the door behind her.

"Are you ready for lunch?" Kara asked. "Is the Seashore Hut deli still around?"

Jeremy raised an eyebrow. The Seashore Hut had been one of their favorite hangouts in high school and just happened to be down the block from the turtle sanctuary. "You want to see Emily, don't you?"

A grin flashed across her pretty face. "I do. But I'm also a little hungry. And I'm sure Emily and Julia will be as well."

Jeremy spun the whiteboard around so that the photos faced the wall. "We can stop at the deli."

Kara didn't move. The intensity of her gaze had Jeremy stiffening. "Can we bring my father's case file? I'd like to look through it again."

"Don't you have copies at home?"

"I do. However, I didn't bring them with me. And now that we know my mother might be involved…" A pained expression bracketed her eyes. "I'd like to look through the notes and evidence again. Or lack thereof."

Jeremy couldn't blame her. He'd had the same idea. "Let's stop at the records room on our way out."

Hopefully, they would come across a clue that would solve the mystery of who and why her father was murdered and put a stop to the attacks on Kara before it was too late.

SEVEN

As soon as Kara and Jeremy arrived at the Safe Haven Turtle Sanctuary, Emily enthusiastically ushered them through the festively decorated lobby.

An explosion of reds, greens and golds sparkled from streams of garland around the reception desk. Large stockings with colorful turtles glued to the material hung ready to be filled.

A live evergreen tree with colorful turtle ornaments dangling from the branches consumed the space near the gift shop.

"Come on, Mommy—you have to meet the turtles." Emily tugged Kara into an area that had a large tank housing several green sea turtles.

Emily pointed to each turtle and shared what she'd learned earlier in the day. She told them all about how the remarkable creatures had been found and rescued.

Seeing Emily's excitement over the turtles warmed Kara's heart. She'd never imagined herself a mother, opting instead to focus on her career. She and David had agreed on that choice, so when they'd conceived, it had been a surprise for them both. A happy one. David had been so excited when Emily was born that he'd cried.

Kara hadn't known she could love anyone as much as she loved her daughter.

But now she was raising Emily alone.

Without a community to help her. No aunts, uncles or cousins close by.

David had been an only child, like Kara.

The closest thing they had to extended family was the babysitter who was paid to spend time with Emily.

Kara liked Mrs. O'Brien well enough. She was a salt-of-the-earth type, a military man's wife and mother to several military children.

But it wasn't the same as growing up in a place where people loved you and wanted to spend time with you just because.

Her heart ached for all that Emily would miss out on when they left the island.

Determination slid through Kara. When she and Emily left South Padre Island, Kara would find a community like she'd had here growing up. She'd find a small town with a good school system and a thriving church. Kara had fond memories of Sunday school classes and youth group outings.

"Emily, have you said thank you to Julia for spending so much time with you and teaching you about the turtles?" Kara said to her rambunctious four-year-old.

Bouncing on the balls of her toes, Emily beamed. Her dark curls framed her little face and emphasized the blue hue of her eyes. "Thank you, Auntie Julia. This has been the best day ever."

Taken aback by Emily's form of address toward Jeremy's sister, Kara's gaze snapped to Julia's.

Pink dotted the other woman's cheeks. "I hope it's okay I asked her to call me that." Julia grimaced as if she expected Kara to be mad at her.

Considering there was a time when Kara thought they

would be sisters-in-law, she couldn't bring herself to admonish Julia for creating a false sense of familiarity with her daughter. "It's fine. In many cultures friends of one's parents are called auntie and uncle."

Julia's relieved smile sent a ribbon of warmth through Kara.

"This is true," Julia said. "I just hope you know that I'm here for you no matter what." Her gaze slid to her brother, who stood off to the side, quietly conversing with Tarren.

"I appreciate that," Kara said carefully. She gestured to the basket of goodies sitting on the reception desk. "We brought lunch."

"Can we have a picnic on the beach?" Emily asked, her hands clasped together.

"I have tarps and blankets." Julia bounced on her toes much the same way as Emily. "There's a park not far. A picnic lunch on the beach sounds fabulous."

"Fabulous," Kara repeated. She was amused by the attention and appreciated how special Julia was making this time for Emily.

They gathered the men and headed down to the beach park where Julia and Tarren spread out two large tarps and then laid blankets over the top of them. They all sat down and opened the bag of sandwiches from the Seashore Hut deli.

Kara tried to relax, but she was eager to get a look at her father's case files once again. Her mind couldn't stop spinning with possible scenarios. Was there something in those files that they had dismissed that could implicate her mother?

After everyone had finished their sandwiches, Julia, Tarren and Raz took Emily down to the water's edge. As they walked away, Julia was telling Emily about the turtles' nesting in the sand that happened in the spring.

An uncomfortable silence echoed between Kara and

Jeremy as they sat on the blanket. The roar of the rushing waves seemed to amplify the reserved quiet stretching between them.

With a quickening of her pulse, Kara realized there was another kind of closure she needed. Carefully, she asked, "Why did you stop communicating with me?"

"Excuse me?" Jeremy's tone was sharp. He sat with his legs out in front of him and twisted to face her.

She met his shuttered gaze. "You stopped answering my emails."

Anger flashed in his eyes. "Only because you demanded I leave you alone."

She tucked in her chin. Confusion swirled in her brain. "What are you talking about? I did no such thing."

He scoffed. The sound was almost like he was choking. "Don't try to gaslight me. I printed off the email."

Temper flaring, she drew back. "Gaslight you? You have some nerve."

She stood and brushed off the bits of sand that clung to her pants. She counted to ten as a way to calm her racing heart, letting the spurt of anger recede.

"I kept all of your emails and the cards," Jeremy said quietly.

Her heart contracted painfully in her chest. She didn't want to admit that she'd kept all of his notes as well.

Though they had communicated via their computers, they'd also sent each other cards in the mail. Seeing his neat handwriting on an envelope used to fill her with pleasure. Then they'd stopped arriving.

For the longest time, she'd hoped to find one in the mailbox with an explanation. But one never showed up.

Why would he say she'd sent him an email asking him to leave her alone? She'd gone over every one of their email exchanges, looking for some clue as to why he'd ghosted her. It made no sense.

This was a dumb idea to try to find closure in such a hurtful part of her life. Surviving the attacks on her life and finding her father's killer was where she needed to keep her focus.

"It doesn't matter anyway," she said with a weary sigh. "Is there somewhere private where we can go through my father's case file?"

Jeremy stood and braced his feet apart. He adjusted the duty belt on his lean hips. "We can go to my place. If you're okay with Emily hanging out more with Julia."

His place? The thought had her heart speeding up again, but not with anger.

Anticipation raced along her limbs. Though why, she didn't know. "Of course. Emily has really taken to Julia."

Not only Julia but Tarren and Raz.

And Jeremy.

If Kara wasn't careful, she'd find herself taken with Jeremy again.

He turned to face the ocean. Kara looked past his broad shoulders to where Emily and the dog were playing in the water's edge. They jumped over the ankle-high waves before rushing up to the drier sand and Julia and Tarren before racing back out to the waves.

If nothing else was accomplished by this trip, at least Emily would have some good memories.

But Kara wouldn't be satisfied until her father's murderer was caught.

"What's up with the people on that boat?"

The tension in Jeremy's voice had Kara rising to her feet. She watched intently as he strode toward the water's edge, the set of his shoulder's rigid. Her gaze moved past Emily to a small cabin cruiser bobbing in the water about a hundred yards out. A man and a woman standing on the open back stared at them through binoculars.

The woman waved her free arm as if trying to get their attention. Well, she had it. Were they in trouble?

The crackle of electricity sounded close to Kara's ear before something hot pressed against her shoulder. A jolt of pain raced through her limbs. Her whole body contracted in one big muscle spasm just as something sticky was slapped over her mouth.

A scream built inside her chest, but it couldn't escape.

The out-of-place noise of the stun gun firing sent a lightning bolt of adrenaline and fear coursing through Jeremy.

He whirled around to see a behemoth of a man wearing an ill-fitting ski mask. He was attempting to carry Kara away from the beach park.

Kara kicked and thrashed, but her efforts proved useless against the giant who had her tucked under one arm like a football. In his other hand he held a double-action revolver aimed at Jeremy.

"No!" Jeremy yelled as he rushed forward, stepping over the stun gun that had been discarded in the sand near the blanket where Kara had been sitting.

The assailant waved the revolver. "Don't follow, man. I'll have to hurt her if you do."

The familiarity of the voice had Jeremy increasing his speed. "George Watkins!"

George hesitated, then increased his pace while trying to hang on to a thrashing Kara.

To Jeremy's right, Raz zipped past. The German shepherd launched into the air and clamped his powerful jaws around George's forearm, sinking his teeth into the tender flesh.

George let out a scream, dropping both Kara and the handgun as he swung Raz in an attempt to dislodge the dog from his arm.

Tarren caught up to Jeremy and yelled, "Out."

Raz immediately released his bite, landing easily on the ground, and backed up until he was standing as a barrier between a sobbing George, who held his bloody arm with his other hand, and Kara, who sat on the ground gripping her shoulder.

Jeremy went to Kara as Tarren wrestled George to the ground and into handcuffs.

"Kara, I've got you." Jeremy gathered her to his chest.

"My shoulder," she groused.

Jeremy eased his hold. Keeping one arm around her waist, he used his free hand to radio for an ambulance.

"Mommy!" Emily's cry drew Jeremy's attention.

Julia carried the little girl toward them. There was no mistaking the concern etched on his sister's face or the tears streaming down Emily's cheeks.

Jeremy held up a hand. "She's okay."

Kara tapped his arm. "Help me up."

"Easy now." He hoisted her to her feet.

She threw him a glance. "You know that guy?"

"I do." He watched as more police arrived and took George into custody, yanking the ski mask from his head and confirming what Jeremy already knew. "He's local. Lots of trouble."

Kara grunted. "I want that man in an interrogation room."

Of course she did.

Jeremy was glad to see her spark hadn't been dimmed by the stun gun. "We'll get to that as soon as your shoulder is checked out." He gestured toward the ambulance that came to a halt at the park entrance.

Once he was sure she was truly okay, he'd get to the bottom of why George had just tried to kidnap Kara.

Kara leaned gingerly against the wall, watching Jeremy lean over the suspect and growl, "Come on, George. Do yourself a favor. Tell us what we want to know. Why did you try to kidnap Agent Evans-Mitchell?"

The suspect, George Watkins, sat in a metal chair, his hands cuffed to a ring attached to the center of the metal table. His dark eyes shifted in her direction.

Her stomach knotted. Why had the man attempted to abduct her? She forced herself to stay silent. This was Jeremy's show, but she itched to jump in with questions.

After having the minor burn on her shoulder doused with antibiotics and bandaged by the paramedics who'd arrived on the scene, Jeremy had driven them to the South Padre Island police headquarters, where she'd joined Jeremy in the interrogation room.

George's wide shoulders slumped. "Agent? No one told me she was an agent."

"Who hired you?" Jeremy probed.

"I told you I don't know," George whined. "A friend asked if I wanted to make some quick cash. He gave me a cell phone and said to answer when it rang."

"And..."

The irritation in Jeremy's tone matched the annoyance growing in Kara's gut.

"The guy on the phone told me there was a car and supplies waiting for me in front of my house with instructions. For five thousand dollars, I was supposed to grab the woman." He darted a glance at her again. "I was to take her to the amusement park."

"How'd you know which woman to take?" Jeremy asked.

"There was a picture of her with the stuff in the car," George replied.

"What friend hooked you up with the phone?" Kara interjected, hoping this *friend* would be more helpful.

George stared at her. "Benny. He said he'd done some work for these guys, and they paid well."

"Benny Basher?" Jeremy asked.

She blew out a frustrated breath and shared a look with Jeremy.

Benny Basher was one of the victims on Jeremy's whiteboard. What was the connection to her father's murder?

"Yeah." George looked hopeful. "Benny knows more than me."

"What can you tell us about Benny?" Kara asked.

George shrugged. "I haven't seen him in a few days. Not since he gave me the phone. He works odd jobs when he's not plastered."

"We can't ask Benny," Jeremy said. "I'm sorry to tell you but your friend is dead."

George tried to stand, but the cuffs attached to the table forced him back into the seat. "What! Am I next?"

Jeremy put a hand on his shoulder. "Settle down, George."

"I'm being set up," he complained.

Kara shook her head. "Dude, you used a stun gun on me and then held the police chief at gunpoint. What part of that would indicate you're being set up?"

Dropping his head into his hands, George moaned. "This isn't good." He lifted his gaze. "Benny gave Anthony a phone, too."

Kara's heart rate ticked up. This could be the break they needed. "What's Anthony's last name?"

"Kubaik," George replied.

"He's a local," Jeremy supplied. "I'll have an officer pick

him up." He moved to Kara's side. "We've got what we can from George." He cupped her elbow and steered her out of the room. "Hopefully, our forensic tech can get a number off the cell phone."

While he spoke with an officer and gave him instructions to book George and put him in holding as well as to find Anthony Kubaik, Kara headed down the hall to where Julia sat with Emily. Taking her daughter into her arms, Kara sent up a prayer of thanksgiving for God's protection.

But this second attempt to abduct her made it clear whoever killed her father wasn't done with their criminal deeds.

EIGHT

With Emily taking a nap while his parents and Julia stayed with her, Jeremy drove Kara to his apartment in downtown South Padre Island. The two-story shiplap building was within walking distance of the sheriff's department. He couldn't squelch the flutter of anxiety about how she would view his space. He didn't have much furniture—he didn't need a lot. The living room consisted of a comfortable couch, a flat-screen TV and a table with two chairs.

When they entered the one-bedroom apartment, he wasn't surprised Kara zeroed in on the floor-to-ceiling bookshelves he'd installed on either side of the large picture window overlooking the backside courtyard. Their love of the written word had been another thing they'd had in common as preteens and teens. Reading and sports were his way to relax. He wondered what she did to find peace now.

He set the box containing Coach Evans's case file and evidence on the dining table and removed the lid. Peering inside at the familiar stack of plastic bags marked and tagged with the date of the coach's murder, a stab of sorrow arrowed through him as it always did when he dragged out the box.

Kara moved to his side and held out a pair of latex gloves.

He raised his eyebrows.

"I want to open each bag." She slipped a pair of gloves over her slender, unadorned fingers. "I don't want to contaminate anything. But I need to hold everything and examine it. Look at it. It's part of my process."

A process that had resulted in the apprehension of several of the FBI's most wanted.

Jeremy had kept up with her career. She'd made a name for herself in law enforcement and had many accolades attached to her reputation.

He hoped and prayed she'd discover something he hadn't. He nodded and pulled the slick gloves over his fingers.

"Do you have a notepad and pen?"

"I do." He hustled to the kitchen counter, where he kept them by his landline.

"Do you want me to be your scribe?" he asked when he returned.

Kara flashed him a smile that sent a tremor through his knees. "That would be appreciated."

For the next hour, they went through each evidence bag. There wasn't much there: Her father's bloodstained jersey. The pants with shin guards also splattered with his blood. His cleats were marred with packed dirt from the pitcher's mound.

With each item, Kara carefully examined the evidence, holding each item up to the light, peering at it as if what she held in her hand might hold the answers to the secrets they hoped to uncover.

"It's so strange to me that the police at the time couldn't find any witnesses or suspects," she said.

"It was a Sunday morning," he said. "Plus, the baseball diamond is at the back of the school with a twelve-foot fence around it to help keep balls out of the greenspace beyond."

"I don't know why my father was there so early that morning," she said. "He'd already left the house by the time I got up to get ready for church. And my mother—" Kara shook her head. "She'd claimed she didn't know he'd left or why. Now I wonder..."

His heart cramped with sympathy. It hurt to think Laine Evans might have had a hand in her husband's brutal demise. But life was strange, and evil happened.

"We don't know if he was lured there," Jeremy said. "Or if the attack was random. A matter of wrong place, wrong time."

When the box was empty, she stepped back and tilted her head. She held up the crime scene photos. "Do you know what's missing here?"

Jeremy's heart fluttered. "Missing? This is everything that was collected that day."

"His watch. He's not wearing one in these photos. I don't know why it never occurred to me before." Her voice held a note of self-reproach. "My father always wore one of his watches. You saw his box where he kept his collection at the house."

Feeling like he'd been sucker punched, Jeremy said, "I never even thought of his watch. But you're right. He always had one on. The baseball diamond where his body was discovered was thoroughly searched."

"We'll have to go back to the house so I can inspect his watches. I can't say for sure I'll be able to remember them all or know which one is gone, but I need to see them again."

Jeremy's mind whirled with possibilities. "If he was wearing a watch that day and it wasn't found in the vicinity of his body..."

A steely glint shone in her eyes. "The killer took a souvenir."

A shudder ran rampant over his flesh. If only they had a suspect.

"I'm not seeing anything that I could say implicates my mother. Except for the lack of a watch."

But there was a look on her face that told him she'd thought of something. "What?"

Her eyes were wide. "But if my father was wearing a watch when he was killed, it would have his blood on it."

"We should gather the watches and have our forensic team check them for any trace evidence."

Kara replaced all the evidence back into the bags, sealed them before putting them neatly in the box and secured the lid. "How quickly do you think your techs could get to work on the watches?"

He hesitated. They had a small lab with only two techs and three recent murders that needed processing. "I can put a rush on processing them. It might take them a week."

Holding his gaze, Kara said, "Would you be offended if I boxed up all the watches and sent them to the FBI crime lab in Quantico?"

This was too important for him to claim any sort of territorial jurisdiction. "Not at all."

Before leaving his apartment, Jeremy grabbed a shoebox from his closet containing Kara's cards and copies of their email correspondence.

Later, when the time seemed fitting, he'd give them to her, including the last one he'd received telling him to leave her alone.

The one she claimed not to have written.

What was that about? A lapse in memory? Or just denial?

They made short work of going back to Kara's childhood home, carefully placing the collection of watches into individual evidence bags, dating and tagging them with their signatures and boxing them up.

Kara wasn't sure if one was missing. There were several empty slots, which didn't help to narrow down if one was missing. But it wasn't like him not to wear a watch out of the house.

They stopped at the post office, where she mailed the box to the FBI's crime scene techs.

If any of the watches came back with Coach Evans's blood on it, what would it mean?

Jeremy couldn't imagine how Kara was feeling right now, knowing that her mother might have been involved in covering up her father's death.

Kara and Jeremy returned to the Hamiltons' home after dropping off the watches at the post office and arrived in time to say goodbye to Rick and Irene as they headed out for their Bible study group. Then Kara and Jeremy sat down to a delicious dinner with Julia and Emily.

"Thank you for dinner, Julia." Kara helped Jeremy's sister clear the table after their savory dinner of steak and potatoes for the adults. "And thank you for making Emily's favorite—mac and cheese with sliced hot dogs."

"Sometimes a kid just needs to eat like a kid," Julia said with a smile. She still had on her Safe Haven Turtle Sanctuary T-shirt and cargo pants.

Kara joined her in the kitchen to put the dirty dishes into the sink. "You'll make a good mother one day."

Grinning, Julia said, "I'm hoping that while you're here, you can help me with some of my wedding preparations."

Surprise spread through Kara. "You've set a date?"

"March," she said. "Tomorrow I'm supposed to go to the wedding boutique to look at dresses. Would you and Emily care to join me and Mom?"

Grateful and a bit bemused to be included, she asked, "What time?"

"My fitting appointment is at one."

"We should be able to make that."

"And the wedding?"

Julia's query had Kara smiling. "We wouldn't miss it for the world."

"In that case, would you be one of my bridesmaids? And Emily could be my flower girl?"

Oh boy. Kara didn't know the first thing about being a bridesmaid. Or being a bride, for that matter. She and David had been married at the courthouse in downtown Alexandria. Her mother was the only witness.

Feeling a flutter of anxiety, Kara said, "Are you sure? Don't you want a close friend?"

Julia's smile was indulgent. "My maid of honor is one of my best friends. Besides, no matter the distance, you and I will always be friends."

How could she deny Julia? "Of course."

Kara returned to the dining table to grab the platter with the extra barbecued steaks, but her attention was caught by the activity visible out the sliding glass door.

Jeremy, Tarren, Emily and Raz were in the backyard. Kara hesitated as she watched Emily and Raz running around the grassy area. Emily ran to Jeremy and hugged his leg. He picked her up and swung her around before setting her back on her feet. Then Emily took off running, with Raz chasing after her.

With her heart in her throat, Kara trusted that Jeremy would keep her daughter safe from the infinity pool and the ocean beyond. But who would protect both of their hearts?

Her cell phone rang. The caller ID revealed her uncle's name. "Hello, Uncle Don."

"Sorry—I just heard your message," he said. "So, you're in town. Are you staying at your mom and dad's home?"

Her home now. But she didn't quibble. "No, I'm staying

with—" she wondered how much her uncle knew about her and Jeremy and their past "—friends."

She didn't feel the need to get into a discussion about her ex-boyfriend and his family with her uncle.

"Okay. You know you're more than welcome to come here," he said. "I have plenty of room."

Her uncle, a perpetual bachelor, lived in one of the newer high-rise buildings that had cropped up along South Padre's shoreline. He worked for the city in the permit department as a supervisor. She often wondered why he never married.

"Thank you for the offer," she said. "Emily and I would like to see you before we leave. Will you have some time?"

"You're not staying for Christmas?"

"No, just another day or two," she told him. It was on the tip of her tongue to ask him about her parents' marriage, but she held back. She wasn't ready to cast aspersions on her mother until she had more information.

"You know the Christmas festival begins this week," he said. "It would be a shame for Emily to miss it."

Fond memories of viewing the many beautiful sandcastles built along the shore for the annual Holiday Sandcastle Village filled her mind. Sculptors from all over came to the island to exhibit their skill in building and decorating holiday-themed sand art. She knew Emily would find it enchanting.

"Opening ceremonies are tomorrow night," Don said. "How about we meet there?"

"That would be fabulous," she told him.

They agreed on a time and a location to meet. Then she hung up. The back sliding door opened and Emily and Raz rushed through the door and into the living room, where they both plopped down onto the big dog bed in front of the hearth.

Jeremy and Tarren walked in behind them, their faces grim.

Jeremy lowered his voice to say, "We have another dead body. Same MO as the last three victims."

Jeremy brought his vehicle to a halt around the backside of the Oceanside Shopping Center. The night sky was lit up with flashing red and blue lights from emergency vehicles already on the scene.

Beside him, Kara unbuckled her seat belt. "I don't think you can keep this a secret anymore." She pointed to the news van a few yards away.

Jeremy rolled his eyes. Of course the local news station would be in attendance with the location being so public. That the police department had managed to keep the other three murders out of the public's eye was a feat Jeremy had hoped would last until they had some resolution.

He and Kara walked up to the scene where Officer Stacy Ridgefield met them. She was a tall woman with brunette hair that she wore back in a tight bun.

"Kara, this is Officer Ridgefield, who comes to our little bit of paradise by way of Boston," Jeremy said. "And, Stacy, this is FBI Special Agent Kara Evans-Mitchell."

The two women shook hands in greeting.

Stacy then said, "The victim, Anthony Kubaik, was found in the dumpster by two employees."

Kara gasped. "What? Are you sure?"

Stacy held up a photo ID with a gloved hand.

Acid burned in Jeremy's gut. His gaze moved to where two employees, both wearing green aprons and Santa hats, were being interviewed by officers. "Is this the primary scene?"

Stacy shook her head. "No. It looks like it was a body dump."

That would make their job harder. "Single gunshot to the head?"

"Yes, Chief. Like the others," Stacy said.

He met Kara's gaze, saw the same question in her eyes that ran through his head. How were these deaths connected to Coach Evans's murder?

"Doctor Burns arrived a while ago." Stacy referred to the medical examiner. "Detective Rodgers has officers canvassing the area for witnesses."

Kara put her hand on Jeremy's arm. "Look to your left, end of the parking lot."

Jeremy turned, scanning the few cars left in the spaces until his gaze landed on a red pickup truck. His gut clenched. Could that be the same vehicle that had rammed into him and Kara, pushing them into the ocean? From this angle, he couldn't see if the front end had any damage.

To Stacy, he said, "Keep the press at bay. Tell them we'll do a news update once we have more information. Make sure everything is bagged and tagged."

Stacy nodded. "You got it, Chief." She jogged back to where the medical examiner and his assistant were placing the victim in a body bag.

Without having to say a word, he and Kara headed for the red truck. As they drew closer, he put his hand on his holster and unstrapped the safety buckle. He lifted the weapon slightly out of its sheath.

Kara took out her weapon and held it in both hands close to her body.

With caution, they approached the vehicle.

There didn't appear to be anyone in the vehicle. In a half crouch, Jeremy slid up to the back of the truck and peered over the sidewall. The truck bed was empty.

With Kara right beside him, he moved forward to the passenger-side door and peered in through the backside window. Empty. Still, he wasn't taking any chances.

Last year someone had rigged Tarren's vehicle with an explosive device. Jeremy got down onto his knees and looked at the undercarriage of the vehicle, shining his flashlight between the tires.

"Anything?"

"I don't see any explosives." But that didn't mean that there wasn't a device set to blow.

He motioned for Tarren and Raz to join them.

Kara went around to the front of the vehicle. "This is the truck that rammed into us."

Jeremy moved to stand beside her and viewed the crunched front grill.

"What's up?" Tarren and Raz came to a halt beside him.

"This is the vehicle that pushed us into the channel," he said.

Tarren whistled. "Probably abandoned after the incident."

"Maybe," Jeremy agreed. "Let Raz take a whiff."

Tarren gave Raz the command to search. The K-9 went to work. His nose twitched as he and Tarren walked slowly around the vehicle, but the dog showed no sign of anything amiss.

That Raz didn't alert gave Jeremy the confidence to approach the truck door. Keeping his hand on his weapon, he opened the passenger side.

The seat was covered in blood.

Surprise arced through him. "We may have found the primary crime scene."

"Could Anthony be one of the men who ran us off the road and stole the bat? He wore a mask, so I can't identify him." Kara moved to stand beside him. "The same man George mentioned?"

"We'll have to test the blood for a DNA match," Jeremy stated. "But my gut tells me yes."

"He appears around the right height and weight as the masked man who was in my house when I arrived," she said.

"But now he's dead. So if Anthony is the man who stole the bat, then he gave it to whoever hired him, and they killed him for his effort," Tarren pointed out.

Kara met Jeremy's gaze. "But if that is the case, then are all of these murders related? And somehow connected to my father? As well as the kidnapping attempts on me?"

NINE

All they had at this point was conjecture. Theories that might or might not prove to be true about the murders and the attacks on Kara.

Using the radio attached to his shoulder, Jeremy called for the forensic team to meet him at the truck.

Somehow, someway, they would figure it out.

This was going to be a long night.

"I'm going to run the plates through the FBI database," Kara said. "You okay with that?"

Jeremy liked that she beat him to the task. Her resources would probably be faster. "Have at it."

Kara took a picture of the plate with her phone, typed in a message and sent off the image.

By the time the forensic team arrived at the truck and started processing the vehicle, Kara had an answer.

"Have you ever heard of the Mortenson Group?" she asked.

"Of course," Jeremy said.

"They're a big developer here on the island," Tarren supplied. "They built this shopping mall and several of the new high-rise apartment buildings and hotel resorts."

"This truck is registered as a company vehicle," Kara said.

"Now, that is an interesting development," Jeremy said. He'd never met the owner of the Mortenson Group. "In the morning, we'll visit Bob Mortenson and see if we can discover what his company truck was doing here and if our victim worked for him. That is, assuming the blood in the truck matches our victim."

"I can also talk to my uncle," Kara said. "Maybe he would have some information about this Mortenson Group since he works for the city in the permits department."

"It certainly couldn't hurt to know if there's something shady going on with Mortenson. But as far as I know, he's a standup guy. His wife and Mayor Carter's wife are friends. Bob and the mayor play golf."

She slid him a sideways glance. "Do you golf with the mayor?"

Jeremy scoffed. "I'm a city employee. I don't rub elbows with the higher-ups."

"There's not much more we can do here," Kara said. "I'd like to go with you tomorrow to visit the Mortenson Group."

"I would expect nothing less."

After learning from Jeremy that Bob Mortenson was out of town and wouldn't return until the following day to meet with them, Kara called her uncle and asked if she and Jeremy could swing by his office.

They agreed to meet in an hour, at nine in the morning. Because Jeremy's work vehicle was still out of commission, he'd driven his personal SUV and had to park several blocks away from city hall since most of the parking spots were filled.

The town was brimming with tourists and locals alike getting ready for the upcoming Christmas celebration.

Green garland wound around the light poles along the main street, and various Christmas tunes drifted from open storefronts. They passed the local bakery, and the smells of sugar and spice wafting on the air made Kara's stomach grumble.

They'd skipped Jeremy's parents' breakfast spread, each grabbing a banana to eat on the way.

Emily was content to stay with Irene and Julia. Kara was beyond grateful to the Hamilton family for their care and concern for her daughter.

Uncle Don's office was on the top floor of the town hall building, situated in the middle of downtown South Padre Island. He had a nice ocean view.

The office itself wasn't much more than a box with several tall filing cabinets, a desk sporting a large computer monitor plugged into a laptop and a nameplate with *Don Kearns* in gold letters.

After a quick hug, Kara took a seat next to Jeremy, facing the expansive mahogany desk while her uncle sat across from them.

His hair had grayed over the years, turning more salt than pepper. He looked more worn since the last time he'd visited his sister, Kara's mom, in the hospice facility. He had a deep tan from obviously spending time in the sun, but dark circles ringed his eyes. He wore a Rolex wristwatch that she'd seen him wear before and a gold chain around his neck that peeked out from the V of the blue button-down shirt he wore.

"It's really great you're here," Don said. "I wasn't expecting the chance to see you until this evening."

Jeremy turned a questioning gaze to Kara.

"The Holiday Sandcastle Village opens tonight," she said to him. "I was planning to take Emily."

Jeremy didn't say anything but gave a slow nod. It was on the tip of her tongue to tell him that she had intended to ask him to come with them, but it didn't seem like the appropriate thing to do at this precise moment.

Instead, Kara blurted out the question that was burning

a hole in her brain. "Do you know if my mom and dad were having marital difficulties before my father's murder?"

Don's chin dipped. He blinked, and confusion swirled in his deep blue gaze. "Now, that's a thing to ask. Why, after all this time, would you want to know something like that?"

"I'm curious," Kara said. "Mom—" She paused. What had her mother said? She'd never talked about her husband or his murder. Kara had always assumed she still grieved the loss. But now...

"Your mother, what?" Don's sharp tone was a surprise. "What did she say?"

Kara shook her head. "She wouldn't say anything. She never wanted to talk about Dad."

Don splayed his hands on the desk. "Kara, honey, you need to let that go. It was a long time ago. Whoever hurt your father—"

"Murdered my father," Kara insisted.

Don inclined his head. "Murdered. They're probably long gone by now." He shifted his gaze to Jeremy. "Isn't that right, Chief?"

"The case is still open," Jeremy said carefully.

"Is that what you're doing here?" Don's gaze bounced between Jeremy and Kara, then lingered on her. "What happened to your face?"

Refraining from touching the still-visible bruises on her cheek and jaw, one from her scuffle with the intruder at her house and the other from being punched by the man who stole the bat, she replied, "There was a break-in at the house. I interrupted the burglar. And then—"

Don's eyes flared and concern creased his brow as he interjected, "Why didn't you call me? This is so weird. I had a break-in a few weeks ago."

Kara's gaze jumped to Jeremy.

"I heard about it," Jeremy said. "From what I remember, there was a rash of break-ins at the time in the apartment building you live in. We arrested the teenage son of one the tenants."

"True. But his parents swear he's not guilty," Don said, focusing back on Kara. "I can't believe you were hurt. Did the intruder take anything?"

"Not then," she said. The intruder hadn't found what he was looking for that night.

Don frowned. "Meaning?"

She glanced at Jeremy, silently asking if she should mention the bat. He gave a small nod of his head.

"Later, we did find something." Her heart pounded in her chest. "We found the bat that was used to kill my father."

Don sat back. His tanned face lost color. "Where?"

"In the false bottom of my mother's hope chest."

"I didn't know she even had that still." He sat forward. "Where's the bat?"

"It was stolen from us," she said.

Don rubbed a hand over his chin. "It's gone. Wow. This is unbelievable. Who?"

"We don't know," Jeremy said. "But we intend to find out."

Deciding to steer the conversation in the direction they'd come to discuss, she asked, "Uncle Don, what can you tell us about the Mortenson Group?"

Her uncle's eyebrows rose. "Why would you be asking about the Mortenson Group?"

"The company came up in an investigation," Jeremy supplied. "We're just doing our due diligence."

Don's gaze narrowed slightly as his eyes shifted from Kara to Jeremy and back to her. "'We'? Aren't you out of your jurisdiction? Does the FBI have authority here?"

Kara wasn't surprised by the question. Her uncle was part

of the city of South Padre Island's governing body. It would seem odd to him that local law enforcement would work with the FBI without some sort of official declaration.

"I'm here on vacation, but I am consulting with Jeremy. Unofficially."

Don sat back as realization dawned on his face. "Of course. I'd forgotten. You two were an item at one time."

"Ancient history," Jeremy said in a tone that didn't invite any more discussion.

Kara hated the hurt that burst inside her chest.

"We would like to get some background information on the Mortenson Group," Jeremy continued.

Don considered, then asked, "Why come to me?"

Kara shrugged. "Mom always said nothing happened on this island that you didn't know about. Has the Mortenson Group had any sort of trouble lately?"

Don frowned and leaned forward, bracing his elbows on the desk and steepling his hands. "Trouble? Not that I know of. Bob Mortenson is a standup guy. He and I go way back. He was a friend of your father's, too."

At the mention of her father, her heart gave a little bump. "How did Dad know Bob Mortenson?"

Don shrugged. "Back then, Bob was an up-and-coming developer. He schmoozed with everybody. It's not like they were best friends or anything. But they knew each other. I mean, it is a small island. Small town. Your father was a public figure in many ways."

"True," Kara said. "So what can you tell us about the Mortenson Group?"

Don sighed. "Nothing. Honestly, as far as I know the Mortenson Group is on the up and up. They check all the boxes every time they file for a permit. I really would like to know what this is about."

"As I said," Jeremy said, "all part of an ongoing investigation."

Narrowing his gaze, Don asked, "Does this have something to do with the murder last night?"

Kara canted her head. "And how did...?"

Don cut her off with "Please. It's been all over the news."

There was no denying the news coverage. "Did you know the victim?"

"Everyone knew Anthony Kubaik," Don said. "He hangs out at the Rusty Sailor most nights. I believe he works on the docks in Corpus Christi."

Kara shared a glance with Jeremy. The Rusty Sailor was a local dive bar and one of the first drinking establishments on the island located near the marina.

Jeremy's phone rang. He glanced at it, then looked at Kara. "It's Mayor Carter. I have to take this."

He got up and walked out of the office.

"Now that he's gone," Don insisted, "tell me what's going on."

"Sorry, Uncle, I'm here as a guest of the South Padre Police Department," she told him. "It's not my place to discuss an ongoing investigation."

Don made a face.

"I need to know what happened to my father."

With a nod, Don asked, "Are we still on for this evening?"

"Yes. I'm sure Emily will enjoy visiting you as well as seeing the Holiday Sandcastle Village."

"Bob Mortenson will be at the opening ceremony," he said. "His company is sponsoring the festival."

"That's good to know," she said. So not out of town as they'd been told. She'd make sure to inform Jeremy. "Do you happen to know where my mom kept her important papers, like her will, the mortgage documents and the like?"

"She didn't take them to Virginia with her?"

"No. She said they were here, but I haven't found them at the house." Frustration made her antsy. She rose from the chair. It was time to get moving. Form a new plan. "Thank you, Uncle. We'll see you tonight."

Don came around the desk to give her a hug. The spicy aftershave he wore overwhelmed her senses and brought tears to her eyes because it was the same scent that her father had once used. She stepped back, blinking the moisture from her eyes.

Don held her hands. "I miss him, too. He was one of my best friends."

She squeezed his hands. "I don't understand why Mom was so eager to leave South Padre Island. Why did she keep the house? I've gone through it, and there's nothing worth saving except some sentimental mementos."

Her uncle stared at her for a moment. "Maybe the memories of your father were just too much for her. My sister was... eccentric at times."

That was an interesting way to describe her mom. She'd changed after Dad's murder, become scattered and had a hard time focusing. Kara hesitated, then added, "Why did she have the bat that was used in Dad's murder? Was she involved?"

Don's forehead furrowed and he shook his head. His expression conveyed the same frustrating lack of answers.

"You never said—do you think she and my father were having trouble in their marriage?"

His expression softened. "Not that I know of. But neither of them would have confided in me. Your dad and I were friends, but he was married to my sister. My allegiance would always be with Laine."

"Of course." Though Kara didn't really understand the sentiment since she lacked a sibling. But knowing how close

Jeremy and Julia were, she could see how complicated it could get if there was trouble in Julia and Tarren's relationship. Jeremy and Tarren had been best friends for as long as Kara had known the Hamiltons. And now Tarren was marrying Julia.

Don walked her to the door. "I hope that you find what you're looking for so that you can have some peace. But spinning your wheels on a more-than-decade-old case, especially now that the evidence is gone, won't bring about the closure you hope to have."

Kara didn't know how she could walk away without closure. But doing so might be her only option.

Jeremy's ears were ringing from the mayor's ranting. When Kara came out of the building and joined him on the sidewalk, he said, "I have to go to the mayor's office this afternoon. He's livid that I didn't tell him that we have a string of connected murders. I'm sure he saw last night's news with Maxwell."

Kara gaped. "Maxwell, as in Max Street?"

"The one and only." The island's investigative reporter had also been a classmate of theirs in grade school and high school.

"Wow." Kara fell into step with him. "I expected him to be off to some big city or some foreign country as a war correspondent. He was always talking about seeing the world."

"If memory serves, he did go abroad as a war correspondent after college, but he came back a few years ago."

"Well, as my uncle said, this is a small island and a small town. Everyone knows everyone and everyone's business."

Jeremy adjusted the cowboy hat on his head. "That may be correct."

"Did you tell Mayor Carter the deaths might be linked to my father's cold case?"

He stepped aside to allow a woman with two kids in tow to pass.

"Those boys were in awe of the chief of police," she said with a wink.

He grinned, liking that way she looked at him, as if she were in awe, too.

Walking again, he resumed their conversation. "In answer to your question, no. Until we have solid evidence that all of this is connected, I'd rather keep that between us."

"We should talk to George again," Kara said. "Maybe he knows more than he's saying."

"Good point."

"I'm going to meet Julia and Emily at the bridal shop at one," she said. "Before then, I'll go visit the Rusty Sailor while you're meeting with the mayor."

"I don't want you going to that place," Jeremy said. He'd lost count of the times the department had been called to send officers over to break up a fight.

"Jeremy, I'm armed, and I can handle myself," she told him. "Don't coddle me."

Jeremy conceded the point by holding up his hands. "Okay. Okay. But I'm sending you with an escort. I'll have Stacy go with you. Promise me you won't take any chances."

She saluted him. "Yes, Chief Hamilton."

He bumped her shoulder. "Hey, you can't blame me for being concerned."

She sobered. "I don't blame you. I'll be careful. And I'll appreciate the backup."

He had to trust her. And trust God to protect her when he couldn't. "It's early enough in the day that maybe the Rusty Sailor won't be too crowded. Let's hope the bartender will have some information we can use."

He took out his phone to call Officer Ridgefield. He explained what they needed and told her he was bringing Kara by so they could go in Stacy's cruiser.

"We can walk to the station." Jeremy steered toward the crosswalk. When the walk sign flashed, they started across the intersection.

The squeal of tires against the pavement grabbed Jeremy's attention. A dark blue sedan pulled away from the curb and barreled straight for them.

TEN

With his heart lodged in his throat, Jeremy reached for his sidearm with one hand while simultaneously pushing Kara out of the way of the sedan racing toward them.

Her arm shot out, and her hand landed on his shoulder and shoved at him.

Using their shared momentum, they both dove in opposite directions seconds before the sedan zoomed through the intersection where they'd been standing.

Jeremy landed on his shoulder with a burst of pain. Ignoring the impact, he twisted, bringing his sidearm up and shooting out the back tire of the sedan.

It careened out of control and slammed into a parked car.

Kara was up and running toward the vehicle before Jeremy was able to check that she was okay.

He ran after her. "Kara, stay back."

Gasoline poured out of the sedan's ruptured gas tank.

She skidded to a halt.

He caught up with her, snaked an arm around her waist and drew her farther away.

She frowned at him. "That guy tried to mow us down."

"Call 911," he said.

She gave a sharp nod.

Trusting her to do as he asked, he stalked forward, careful to stay out of the path of the gasoline. He needed to check on the driver, who was slumped over the steering wheel. The man looked to be in his late twenties, with stringy blond hair down to the collar of his fast-food uniform polo shirt. Blood dripped from a cut on his forehead.

Yanking open the driver's-side door, Jeremy reached in to check the man for a pulse. It was weak and thready, but the man was alive. Jeremy did not recognize him, but he rarely visited the local fast-food joint.

A scream rose in the air.

He whipped around to see a man wearing a bandana around the lower half of his face and dark sunglasses covering his eyes, grabbing Kara and lifting her off her feet. He managed to drag her into the open side door of a white panel van.

Abandoning the driver and the wrecked car, Jeremy raced to help Kara.

Meeting her gaze, he shouted, "Drop."

He prayed she would understand, and was thankful when she went limp in the man's arms, providing a clear shot.

Jeremy fired, winging her captor.

The man let her go, and she tumbled out of the van and onto the ground.

She twisted to a sitting position with her sidearm raised as the van door slid shut. The van's engine revved seconds before the vehicle burned rubber as it fled down the street. Kara fired into the back panel window. It exploded in a shower of glass, leaving glittering pieces on the pavement as the van sped away.

Jeremy reached Kara and helped her to her feet.

"They're determined," she groused as she holstered her weapon beneath her dark green blazer.

Frustration burned in his gut. "Why is someone trying to kidnap you?" He pushed his hat back. "What do they want?"

"When we catch 'em, we'll ask 'em." Her gaze drifted to the wrecked car. "Seems the driver was okay, yeah?"

Jeremy turned to see the driver's seat now empty. The driver must've come to and escaped.

A growl of frustration rose in his chest. He'd find the guy later. "Come on, let's get you out of here."

Staying alert, he hustled her to the police station. Once inside, he let out a breath. She was safe here.

Aware of Kara following him, he explained the situation and gave orders to his officers.

"Someone go down the street to the wrecked car. Get Forensics there. The guy didn't have gloves on. We need a name on the driver." He gave them the name of the fast-food joint that was on the logo of his shirt.

Seeing Stacy, he beckoned her to follow him and Kara into his office.

Jeremy rounded his desk to face the two women. "Stacy, I need you to stay with Kara. She is never to be left alone."

Kara opened her mouth, no doubt to protest.

He held up a hand, stalling her. "This is how it's going to be, Kara. You will not be left alone again."

She clamped her lips together with a nod. "What about the Rusty Sailor?"

"I'll send an officer," Jeremy said. "But you're not going anywhere near the place."

She stared at him for a moment, and he wondered if he would get pushed back. Then she nodded again.

"I have a date with your sister and my daughter." She turned to Stacy. "You want to go bridal-gown shopping?"

Stacy's eyes widened, and her gaze darted from Kara to Jeremy.

"My sister's the bride. Tarren's the groom," he stated quickly.

The last thing he needed was a rumor going around that he was getting married to Kara. Not that the idea didn't appeal, but letting his mind or heart ever drift down that path again wasn't a good idea.

"Ahh," Stacy said. "Of course. Tarren's been walking around for months with a goofy grin."

Kara flashed him an amused smile.

Officer Daniel Fribes stuck his head into the room. "Chief, we found the safe-deposit box."

Jeremy waved him into the office. "Daniel, come in."

"We found the bank over in Corpus Christi," Daniel said as he walked in carrying a metal box. "Hope it's okay, but I had a judge sign off on a warrant." He held up the box. "I haven't opened it. I thought you would want to do the honors." He moved forward and placed the box on Jeremy's desk.

Kara rushed forward. The two officers hung back.

Jeremy moved to stand next to Kara.

Her hands trembled as she lifted the lid.

Inside the metal box was a stack of papers. Holding the papers in place was a sand dollar–size key-chain charm in the shape of a colorful turtle.

Jeremy didn't know much about precious stones, but it looked as if the turtle was made of something expensive. "Is that real?"

Kara lifted the turtle from the box and studied it. "Jade. Not costly. This belonged to my father and held the school keys on it."

Why had Laine Evans thought the turtle charm important enough to keep in her safe-deposit box?

Kara reached inside and pulled out the papers.

Looking through them, she breathed out a sigh. "These are the documents I've been looking for." She lifted her confused gaze to his. "Why didn't she just tell me about the safe-deposit box instead of having me search the house for no reason?"

"At least you have them now," he said, unable to give her the answer she sought.

"Do you think she wanted me to find the baseball bat?" She made a face. "A guilty conscience?"

Dropping the key-chain charm into her suit jacket pocket, she asked, "Do you have an envelope I can put these in?"

He grabbed one from his desk.

She placed the documents in the envelope and secured it with the brass fastener. "I'll get these to Joyce at the real estate office on the way to the bridal shop."

Directing his attention to Stacy, he said, "I'm entrusting her and my family to your safety."

"I won't let you down," Stacy said.

Watching the women leave, Jeremy's heart pounded. He still had a meeting with Mayor Carter to get to.

And a mystery to solve.

Why was someone so determined to kidnap Kara? What did they hope to gain from her? How did the string of murders connect to her father's cold case? What did the Mortenson Group have to do with any of this?

Focusing on the remaining officer, Jeremy said, "Where's Rodgers?"

"He's canvasses for witnesses in the Kubaik case," Daniel replied.

"I want you to work with Detective Rodgers. We have four murder victims. At least one is connected to the Mortenson Group. See if you two can find out if the other three victims had any personal connection to the company or to Bob Mortenson. Also, go see George Watkins and ask if he's done any work for the Mortenson Group."

"You got it, boss." Daniel hustled away.

Jeremy wasn't sure how this would all play out, but he knew so much of police work was a waiting game.

Right now, he had to focus on figuring out how to keep Kara safe.

After dropping the necessary papers off at the real estate office, Kara entered the bridal shop with Stacy at her heels. She wasn't used to having a bodyguard, but it was better than taking chances.

Inside the shop, Irene Hamilton, dressed in a light yellow linen pantsuit, and Emily, dressed in another Christmas dress—this one white with a *Nutcracker* motif—sat on a wide, light pink, rhinestone-encrusted settee.

Emily jumped up and ran over to wrap her arms around Kara's legs.

"Mommy, look at all the pretty dresses." Emily beamed up at her and made a sweeping gesture with her hand.

Reaching down to pick up her daughter, Kara settled her on her hip. "They are certainly pretty."

For her own wedding, she'd opted for a tea-length vintage dress for their courthouse ceremony. A happy time that ended much too soon.

Her heart pounded. Was she ready to move on? To give her heart again?

Jeremy's image rose in her mind, and she quickly dispelled the idea that she could ever trust Jeremy not to demolish her heart for a second time. Trusting him with their lives wasn't nearly as scary.

Focusing on the here and now, she gestured to the uniformed officer standing beside her and said, "This is Stacy. She's going to hang out with us today."

Emily's eyes widened. "You're a peace officer."

Stacy, who was dressed in her South Padre Island police

uniform, smiled and nodded. "I am. Keeping the peace is what I do best."

Emily squirmed to get down. Her leg snagged on the charm inside of Kara's suit pocket. "Ouch."

Setting Emily on her feet, Kara withdrew the turtle-shaped key chain.

"Oh, that's pretty," Emily cooed.

"It was your grandpa's," she said. "Would you like it?"

"Yes, please." Emily held out her hands.

Kara placed it in her sweet little palms. "You have to take care of this."

Holding the charm close to her chest, Emily said reverently, "I will, Mommy."

She ran to show it to Irene.

"How lovely," Irene said. "Should we attach it to your backpack?"

Emily grabbed her pink backpack and held it while Irene secured the key-chain charm to the outside zipper of the large pouch on the backpack.

Touched by how good Irene was with Emily, Kara's heart swelled with affection.

The fitting room door opened and Julia walked out wearing a beautiful A-line wedding dress.

"Oh, Julia." Irene clasped her hands together.

Kara joined her daughter on the settee as they watched Julia try on dresses, which was a wonderful distraction. A deep sense of belonging spread through her chest. She wanted Emily to have this sort of connection to women who loved her.

But it wasn't lost on Kara that Stacy placed herself between the shop door and the large picture window. She was taking her job seriously, and Kara appreciated the protection. She just wished she understood why she needed it.

* * *

Jeremy had a headache brewing by the time he finished up his appointment with the mayor and left city hall. He'd given Mayor Carter as much information as necessary without highlighting the connection to the Mortenson Group. Jeremy needed to be mindful that the mayor and Bob Mortenson had a personal friendship.

He would not cast aspersions on the mayor's friend until he had something concrete. For all Jeremy knew, the connection to the Mortenson Group was a fluke or a peripheral, minor detail in the grand scheme of things.

When he arrived back at his office, Daniel and Detective Rodgers were waiting for him.

Rodgers went first. "I talked to the bartender at the Rusty Sailor. All of our victims were patrons, and the four men worked on different construction crews for the Mortenson Group. The bartender said they'd been acting strange for the last couple of weeks."

Daniel spoke up. "That tracks with what we learned from George. He said that his friends Benny and Anthony were day laborers when they were sober enough. I pulled the financials of all four men, and they were on the Mortenson Group payroll."

Jeremy mulled over the information. Did any of this connect with Coach Evans's twelve-year-old cold case? More importantly, how did these murders connect to Kara?

The atmosphere of the annual South Padre Island Holiday Sandcastle Village was filled with laughter and the smells of Christmas from the culinary delights the vendors were offering.

From childhood, Jeremy had always loved the festival. There were waffle cones filled with peppermint ice cream and hot chocolate with marshmallows, even though it was in the low seventies. Who didn't love hot chocolate and peppermint ice cream any time of the year?

Watching Emily as she darted from one sand-sculpted creation to the next, sipping from her hot chocolate and coming away with a marshmallow mustache, Jeremy's heart pounded in ways he'd never expected.

A yearning that was unfamiliar crested deep inside. And with Kara next to him, seeing the delight on her face as she watched her daughter, he wished he could keep them close forever.

But he knew that was an impossibility.

Kara was in danger, and he needed to keep his wits about him.

He was thankful Tarren and Raz had their six, along with Stacy and Daniel and several other undercover police officers roaming the area.

He was not going to rob Emily of this experience, nor would he allow anyone to get close enough to Kara or her daughter to cause harm.

Over the loudspeakers, the *tap, tap, tap* of someone attempting to gain everyone's attention brought him and Kara to a halt. They shared a glance. He saw the anticipation of seeing Bob Mortenson for the first time reflected in her eyes.

"Come along, Emily." Kara steered her daughter toward the front of the assembly gathered around the unlit Christmas tree.

The island always flew in a Douglas fir from somewhere in the Pacific Northwest to serve as the community's official Christmas tree. It was decorated with seashells, ribbons and various other local accouterments. For the out-of-towners, there were also traditional candy canes and shiny baubles.

Bob Mortenson stepped up to the podium. He was a barrel-chested man with a sweep of graying hair over a high forehead. He wore a black suit featuring a red Christmas tie decorated with white snowmen. Beside him stood a slender blonde woman in an elegant green dress, and next to her stood two towheaded boys, twins, in matching snowman Christmas sweaters and black pants.

"We are proud to host so many great sand sculptors and welcome you to our slice of paradise. Your creations are spectacular, and I speak for everyone at the Mortensen Group as we applaud your creativity. Well done." Bob nodded to the mayor. "Now, Mayor Carter, let's light this tree."

Mayor Carter stepped up to the podium with the ends of two electrical cords in his hands. His white Christmas sweater sported an image of Rudolph the Red-Nosed Reindeer with his nose lit up with a bright red bulb. He leaned into the microphone to say, "Merry Christmas, South Padre Island."

He firmly attached the two electrical cords with a flourish, and the tree lit up to the crowd's cheers.

"Mommy, my backpack!" Emily pulled at her mother's hand. "I left it by the hot-chocolate stand."

"We'll go find it," Jeremy told her, hating to see Emily upset.

He turned to let Tarren know, who, along with Raz and Julia, stood behind them.

"We heard," Tarren said. "We'll come with."

Grateful, Jeremy nodded and ushered them through the crowd to the hot-chocolate stand, but Emily's backpack was nowhere to be found. He asked the people working the booth, but they didn't recall seeing it.

They retraced their steps from the ice-cream stand through the maze of sand sculptures, but there was no pink backpack to be had. His heart ached at how disappointed little Emily was. He hoped there wasn't anything worthwhile inside, but to a child everything was important. They stopped by the registration booth and asked them to keep an eye out if anyone turned it in.

Holding her daughter's hand, Kara said, "I'm sorry, honeybee."

Jeremy knelt down to eye level with Emily. "We can keep looking."

Her big blue eyes stared into his and her lower lip quivered. Was she going to cry? He wasn't sure he would know what to do if she did.

"Are you looking for this?" a deep, familiar voice said from behind them.

Reflexively, Jeremy picked up Emily and held her close as everyone turned to find Kara's uncle Don standing there with Emily's pink backpack dangling off his finger.

"You found it! Thank you, Uncle Don." Emily squirmed to get down.

Jeremy set her on her feet.

She wrapped her arms around Don's legs and hugged him. Then she grabbed her backpack.

Kara tilted her head. "How did you know it was hers?"

Don gave her a disbelieving look. "Her name and address are on the back in the little window."

She seemed to relax. "Right. But how did you find it?"

"I saw you guys leaving the hot-chocolate stand when I went to get my own cup, and I spotted it lying there in the grass. I thought I'd wait until after the tree-lighting ceremony to find you."

"Mommy, I lost the key chain," Emily wailed. Big fat tears pooled in her eyes.

"Key chain?" Don asked. "I didn't see a key chain. Could it be inside?"

Emily ripped the backpack open, pulling out coloring

books and crayons, a snack pack and a juice box. "It's not here."

Kara bent down and helped her put everything back into the backpack. "It's okay, honeybee. We'll try to find you another one."

"But you said that one belonged to Grandpa," Emily whined.

"Grandpa?" Don asked.

Kara helped Emily put the backpack over her shoulders. "We found my mother's safe-deposit box. The turtle key chain was inside, along with all the papers I was looking for. It used to be my father's and held his school keys."

Jeremy once again knelt down to eye level with Emily. Using the pad of his thumb, he wiped away Emily's tears. "I have photos of your grandpa at my parents' house. Would you like to see them?"

"Yes, please." Emily wiped at her tears. "Can we see Santa first?"

Jeremy chuckled. "Of course. We must have our priorities." He rose and said to Kara, "Before we head to Santa, I want to introduce myself to Bob Mortenson."

And get a feel for the man who may know something about their murder victims.

ELEVEN

Standing on the edge of the crowd, still in awe over the large, lit-up Christmas trees, Jeremy held Kara's gaze. He saw the conflict in her blue eyes. She wanted to go with him, but she also wanted to stay with Emily.

He recognized the moment she made her decision. Her daughter took priority.

She took Emily's hand. "We'll wait here."

Tarren gave Jeremy a nod, indicating he and Raz would stand guard. Julia engaged Emily in a conversation about the decorations on the big tree.

"Mind if I go with you?" Don fell into step with Jeremy.

Not sure why Don felt the need to accompany him, Jeremy shrugged. Though he'd said he and Bob were friends. "Sure."

They came to a halt where Bob Mortenson and Mayor Carter and their families stood talking.

"Ah, Chief Hamilton. I thought I saw you in the crowd," Mayor Carter said. He held out his hand for Jeremy to shake. "I didn't realize you had a family."

"A borrowed one, for now."

Don shook hands with the mayor and Bob.

Jeremy turned his attention to Bob, his twin boys on either side of him. He held out his hand. "Mr. Mortenson. I look forward to our meeting tomorrow morning." He'd been told by the Mortenson Group receptionist that Bob was out of town tonight, but he didn't want to cause tension by mentioning it.

Bob gave Jeremy's hand a firm shake. "Chief."

Mayor Carter frowned. "Why do you have a meeting set up with Bob?"

The man waved away the mayor's concern. "It's all right, Jeff. I understand from my executive assistant that you have questions regarding some of our employees."

"That I do," Jeremy said. "I will see you bright and early tomorrow." He nodded his head to the mayor. "Always good to see you, Mayor."

Leaving Don chatting with the two men, Jeremy made his way back to Kara and the others. His phone buzzed in his pocket. He pulled it out and saw that it was Vivian from the crime scene lab. "Vivian."

"Hey, boss. I have that old laptop up and running if you and Agent Evans-Mitchell want to try to get into it."

Hoping the laptop would provide some answers, Jeremy asked, "How late will you be there?"

"I was headed out, but I can stay," Vivian said.

"Leave the laptop on my desk," he told her.

"I can do that." Vivian clicked off.

He replaced his phone in his pocket and joined the group. "Who's ready to see Santa?"

"Me!" Emily busted out.

Jeremy laughed, amazed at the resilience of children.

With Emily skipping along next to Raz, who had no trouble keep up with the child, the adults followed closely behind and headed for the colorfully lit-up boardwalk where a Santa was stationed. They joined a line of kids and parents.

Kara bumped him with her shoulder. "How'd it go?"

"Mortenson acknowledged our appointment in the morning. Also, Vivian called to say the laptop is ready for us to look at."

Anticipation shone in her eyes. "Once we get Emily settled at your parents, can we go?"

He bumped her shoulder back. "Of course. I figured as much."

"Mommy, look—a Christmas tree on the beach." Emily pointed toward the shore where a large tree shone brightly in the night, decorated in white lights, gold garlands, seashells and a shiny bright star on top.

"It's lovely," Kara commented.

Jeremy thought she was lovely. His heart ached with longing. He had to turn away in case she saw the emotions written on his face.

Jeremy drove them back to his parent's house, with Tarren, Julia and Raz following in Tarren's vehicle.

Once they were inside the house, Jeremy pulled out a photo album with pictures from his baseball days with Kara's father. It was a walk down memory lane that evoked both happy and sad emotions. Emily seemed more interested in seeing the pictures of her mother when she was young.

"Okay, that's enough for tonight," Kara said eventually. "Let's get you ready for bed."

A little while later, Emily ran back into the living room. She skidded to a halt in front of Jeremy "Will you read me a bedtime story?"

His heart bumped against his ribs. He'd never read to a child before. "Uh, sure."

Kara patted his arm. "You'll do fine."

Allowing Emily to tug him into the guest room, she grabbed two books off a stack sitting on top of an open suitcase with clothes spilling out.

He smiled to see Kara was still a bit messy. Helping Emily

up onto the bed and beneath the covers, Jeremy sat on the edge of the blue-and-white comforter, careful not to put his dirty, sandy shoes on the bed.

He made it through the first book and halfway through the second before he noticed that Emily's eyes had drifted closed and she was softly snoring. Touched beyond reason that she'd asked him to perform such a wonderful ritual, he leaned in and kissed her forehead before carefully moving off the bed, turning out the light and shutting the door behind him.

"She's fast asleep," he told Kara as she met him in the hallway.

"Thank you," she said softly. "You didn't have to do that, you know."

"It was my pleasure. Honestly," he said, putting all his sincerity into his voice.

She put a hand on his chest. "You're a good man, Jeremy Hamilton."

He captured her hand, brought it to his lips and kissed her knuckles. "Emily is easy to love."

Extracting her hand, she nodded and stepped back. "Let's go check out that laptop."

With Jeremy at her side, Kara stepped into the quiet police station. The desk sergeant gave them a nod as they passed and headed for Jeremy's office. A box labeled *Confidential* sat on the desk. Apprehension and anticipation flooded her veins. Inside the box was her father's laptop that Vivian had managed to charge. Now it would be up to Kara to enter the correct password and see what information of her father's the device held. She hoped the laptop would provide some clues as to why he'd been murdered.

Feeling like they were in a fishbowl with three of the four

walls being windows, she asked, "Can we go somewhere more private to do this?"

"My apartment?"

They would be alone and out of prying eyes at his place. "That would work." She'd been surprised by how minimalistic his apartment had been. Then again, he was a bachelor and, according to Julia and his mother, rarely dated. Not that she had asked them, but rather, they'd volunteered the information while Julia had been trying on wedding gowns.

She'd reminded the two women that she and Emily would return to Virginia soon. But she again promised to come back for Julia and Tarren's wedding in March.

As they climbed into Jeremy's SUV, Kara settled the confidential box on her lap as she noted the various other cars and trucks on the street. Had they been there when she and Jeremy had arrived?

While keeping a tight grip on the box, she kept an alert eye on the side-view mirror. As far as she could tell no one was tracking them as they made their way to Jeremy's apartment building. He parked in a covered spot near the entrance.

Before they climbed out of the vehicle, Jeremy reached to the back passenger floorboard and picked up a shoebox, the same one she'd seen him grab from his apartment when they were there the last time.

Curious, she said, "Care to share?"

He popped open his door. "Inside."

Well, that was cryptic. Curiosity had her eyeing the box in his hands. She carried the box containing the laptop up to his second-floor apartment and set it on the dining table, then opened the lid of the box and took out the large square computer.

Back in the day, the device had been considered top-of-the-line. But now it was a dinosaur. She opened the laptop to find the home screen populated with file folders. She pulled up a chair and sat down.

Her hands trembled slight as she clicked on a folder labeled *House* and found the same documents that had been discovered in the safe-deposit box.

There were folders for various years that her father had coached the high school baseball team. Down in the corner, there was an icon for a folder labeled *Don*.

From over her shoulder, Jeremy asked, "Why would your father have a folder with your uncle's name on it?"

"Let's see." She clicked on it.

The documents contained within were surprising. Apparently, her father and Don, along with Bob Mortenson, had invested in several pieces of property.

Jeremy pointed to the address of one piece of property. "That's where the shopping mall went in about ten years ago."

She pointed to another address on one of the documents. "And this is Don's home address."

Jeremy brought over his personal laptop, took the seat next to her and quickly did some digging online. "The Mortenson Group developed the shopping mall and the apartment complex, plus the strip of land that now houses several high-rise hotels and resorts."

Kara opened another file folder marked *Family*. Pictures populated the screen. Most of the photos were of her growing up through the years. Unexpected emotion swelled within her. Tears streamed down her face by the time she was done scrolling through the photographs and an ache pounded at her temples.

Jeremy handed her a tissue. She gratefully took it. She brought up a picture of her, her father and Jeremy, dated two weeks before her father's murder.

"We had just won the regional championship," Kara said. "Dad was so proud of the way you played."

Jeremy put his arm around her. "He was proud of you, too."

She snorted. "He put me on shortstop that day. I wanted to pitch."

"I'm sorry for that," Jeremy said softly.

She shook her head. "No, it was the right thing to do. There were scouts in the audience. They all came to see you. You could've gone pro."

Jeremy withdrew his arm and stood up. "I lost my passion for baseball after your father's death."

She tracked his graceful movements across the room. He'd always had a lean physique. Tall and trim. Athletic. She used to love to watch him play sports, whether baseball, basketball or surfing the tides of the island.

He retrieved the shoebox from the end table in the living room. "Here, I want you to see this."

Pressure built in her chest, increasing the throbbing behind her eyes as he handed the shoebox to her.

Nausea rolled through her. Her head pounded. She set the box on the table. "You know, on second thought, can we look at this later? I'm not feeling well."

"That's fine." He rubbed at the back of his neck. "I'm getting a headache—"

A shrill sound screamed through the apartment.

Kara's heart rate kicked into overdrive. "What *is* that?"

"It's the carbon-monoxide alarm."

Jeremy spun toward the sound emanating from his bedroom. He hurried to his room, with Kara on his heels.

The carbon-monoxide alarm situated behind the bedside table continued to blare. He quickly disabled the monitor. "Strange that the one in the living room hasn't gone off."

"Do you think it just needs new batteries?" Kara asked.

"Possibly. But I change them out every six months." Nausea roiled in his stomach. Noting her face had drained of color, he said, "Let's get out of here."

They hurried to the living room. Kara grabbed the laptop and the shoebox. They headed toward the door.

Jeremy reached for the knob.

"Wait!" Kara yelled.

He paused to look at her. The blue of her eyes deepened with apparent concern, and the purple hues seemed more pronounced.

"Look at the handle," she said. "It's glowing."

The doorknob shimmered. Cautiously, he put his hand near the metal and felt heat emanating off the gold-plated knob.

A black tube poking through the doorjamb snagged his attention.

Someone was piping in carbon monoxide.

No doubt in hopes to knock them out so that they could kidnap Kara.

Not while he had breath left in his body. He grabbed the tubing, pinching off the noxious, invisible gas. He gave the tubing a tug, but it wouldn't move. This wasn't a permanent option.

They needed fresh air ASAP. "The windows."

Kara was already there trying to open the pull-up window frame. "It's been nailed shut. From the inside!"

A sense of violation invaded his chest, but he would deal with that later. Right now, he needed to get them away from the deadly gas filling his apartment.

"Back in the bedroom."

They hurried into the bedroom and slammed the door shut. He tried the bedroom window, but it had been nailed shut as well. Rather than taking precious time to find a hammer to pry the nails out, he picked up the bedside table lamp.

Holding the brass stick like a bat, he reared back and swung, letting go of the lamp and letting it fly toward the glass pane.

It struck the window with a loud crescendo, sending shards of glass out into the courtyard two stories below. Fresh air rushed into the room.

Jeremy filled his lungs. He hadn't realized how foggy his mental capacity had become in the past few minutes.

From the front living room, they heard a crash as somebody broke down the front door.

Setting the laptop and the shoebox on the floor, Kara faced the door with her sidearm at the ready. "Do we take a stand?"

As much as he wanted to confront the criminals who were after her, he wasn't going to risk her life. Getting out of the apartment and to safety was paramount. Emily needed her mother, and Jeremy vowed not to let anything happen to Kara. "No. Go out the window."

Holstering her weapon, Kara hustled to grab the end of his dresser and dragged it in front of the bedroom door.

Ripping the quilt off the bed, he draped it over the edge of the jagged pieces of glass sticking out of the window frame. "Grab the sheets."

Kara didn't waste time. She grasped the top sheet and threw it at him. Then she released the edges of the bottom sheet and quickly carried it over, where she tied the two ends together.

The bedroom door rattled as someone tried to get in.

"That dresser won't last long," she muttered as she draped the sheet out the window.

He wrapped the end of the fitted sheet around the foot of the large oak bed frame and knotted it. "Go."

Kara was halfway out the window. "Hand me the laptop and shoebox."

He grabbed the laptop from the floor. "You get down, and I'll toss it to you."

"Too risky," she said. "I'll take the laptop under my arm."

The bedroom door shuddered as somebody rammed into it. The dresser gave an inch.

Knowing there wasn't time to quibble with her, he handed her the laptop, which she tucked under her arm before disappearing over the ledge of the window and shimmying down their makeshift rope.

Leaving the shoebox behind, Jeremy didn't waste time climbing down the sheet behind her.

From above, the crash of the dresser tipping over as somebody breached the bedroom echoed across the courtyard. Taking Kara by the hand, Jeremy pulled her through the courtyard and out the side gate.

Instead of heading toward his vehicle in case they had somebody out front keeping watch, he pulled her in the opposite direction. They hustled down the street and stayed in the shadow of the trees lining the street until they were able to cross and head toward the police station.

Why was someone after Kara? When would they strike again?

TWELVE

Kara's heart pounded as she paced Jeremy's office while he and his officers went back to the apartment building in hopes of catching whoever was after her.

Why was someone trying to kidnap her? What did they think she knew or had? Were these the same people who had robbed her home in Virginia? Was the intruder she'd interrupted at her childhood home on her first night back on the island a part of this?

Jeremy entered the office with a grim expression on his face that spoke volumes. "They were gone by the time we got back there. I'm having the place dusted for prints, but I'm not sure we'll find any."

"Not surprising. Do you think they were after the laptop?"

"No one knows we have it except for you, me, Tarren and Vivian," he said. "No, this was another attempt to snag you. Whoever orchestrated this anticipated you being there. They must have had my place watched."

The laptop lay on his desk. She pointed to it. "Can you print off all those documents about the property deals?"

"I'll have Vivian do it tomorrow," he said. "I don't think I have a cable that would work for the printer. And I very much doubt this has Bluetooth capabilities."

She conceded the point. "Is there somewhere safe you can leave it until tomorrow?"

He arched an eyebrow. "Besides the fact that we're in the police department headquarters, I do have a safe I'll put it in."

Despite the gravity of the situation, she grinned. "I knew you wouldn't let me down."

He stared at her a moment, then stomped toward her. "I almost let you down. If not for that second carbon-monoxide alarm that they didn't know about, we would both have passed out, and you would be gone."

She touched a hand to his shoulder. "You're always prepared. No matter what. That's what made you a great baseball player and makes you an excellent police chief."

His gaze rested on her face, dropping to her lips. Her breath hitched. It was everything she could do not to lean toward him and offer up her mouth for a kiss. But doing so would be reckless.

Yet she'd played it safe her whole life.

Only with this man had she ever been reckless. Recklessly competing against him for her father's attention, for a spot on the baseball team. Her recklessness had ended up with her falling in love with Jeremy, only to have her heart broken.

But that was then. She was an adult now and capable of acting without letting her heart break.

She decided being reckless in this moment wasn't a bad thing. Before she could talk herself out of it, she went onto tiptoe and slipped her arms around his neck, pulling him close for a kiss.

The moment Jeremy's lips touched Kara's, his whole body froze and ignited at the same time. Was this really happening? He'd dreamed of this moment so often over the years, even more so since she'd resurfaced in his life. But before, he'd always envisioned a kiss of revenge, one that said, *See what you missed out on?*

But now he'd spent time with her and was getting to know her as an adult. His admiration and respect for her was undeniable, as was his attraction. He realized how much he'd missed her and wished things had turned out differently.

He deepened the kiss, reveling in the sensations rocketing through him, the way his heart seemed to knit back together one second at a time.

A knock at the door had them scrambling apart.

Jeremy turned, ready to growl at whoever stood in the doorway, but his gaze landed on Tarren and Raz. He'd called his friend and asked him to meet him there. He could hardly berate him for doing as he had been instructed.

Reality set in. He'd kissed Kara. What had he been thinking?

Running a hand through his hair, he waved Tarren in with his free hand.

"We had your place tested. No prints beyond yours and Kara's. They'd wiped the place down when they broke in earlier. The carbon-monoxide alarm in the living room had been disabled."

Just as he'd suspected.

"They're getting desperate," Kara said.

"This has to have something to do with Bob Mortenson and his company," Jeremy said.

He relayed the information that his two officers had given him earlier about the four recent murder victims being on the Mortenson payroll.

"I think we should talk to Uncle Don again before the meeting with Bob Mortenson," she said. "Let's find out if we can gain any insight into these property investments that he, my dad and Bob were involved in."

"Agreed." Jeremy turned to Tarren. "You good to follow us back to my parents'? And can you stay the night? We could use Raz's special skills."

Tarren nodded. "Julia is already there. We'll be one big happy family."

Jeremy's heart twisted. If only that were true.

He slanted a glance at Kara. She was biting her lip. A nervous habit he hadn't seen since they were kids. Had the reference to them all being one big happy family affected her as much as it did him?

Or was it the kiss they'd shared that had her so anxious?

He had to get a grip. He couldn't let the circumstances break down the defenses he'd worked so hard to erect. Kara had made it clear she was leaving and not returning once they solved her father's cold-case murder. In his bones, he knew they were close to finding the answers they sought. Then she would be gone from his life again. And he refused to have a twice broken heart.

After a restless night's sleep, Kara dressed in her navy pants suit and white silk blouse. She glanced out the bedroom window and was happy to see an officer stationed outside of the Hamilton home. Her daughter's safety was paramount, and she appreciated that Jeremy wasn't taking any chances.

Something softened in her chest. And at the same time, a jittery feeling had taken up residence in the pit of her stomach, ever since their kiss. Keeping her emotions in check was proving more difficult every day.

Hoping her appreciation of Jeremy didn't show on her face, she entered the dining room and took a seat at the table. He wore a fresh uniform, and his brown hair was swept back. His smile was guarded. Did he regret their kiss? She nibbled on her lip until awareness had her meeting his gaze.

"Not hungry?" he asked.

"Famished," she replied to deflect from her nerves, then stabbed her fork into a piece of pineapple.

After breakfast, Irene, Julia and Emily set about to Christmas crafting.

"I'll show you how to make snowflakes out of paper," Julia promised. "Since that's the only kind of snow we get here."

Seeing how happy Emily was here with the Hamiltons sent a ribbon of gratitude through Kara. She knew her daughter was in good hands as she and Jeremy drove to Don's office in her rental car.

Don was on the phone when they approached the open door to his office. Kara couldn't hear her uncle's conversation because his voice was too low, but from the tone she could tell he wasn't happy.

When she and Jeremy stepped through the doorway, he abruptly hung up and a smile broke out on his face.

"Sorry—we don't mean to interrupt," Kara said.

Don waved away her apology. "You aren't interrupting anything. I didn't know if I would see you again before you left. Didn't you say you were leaving today?"

Had she? She honestly couldn't remember. "I'm staying a few more days. There are some things that we need to wrap up."

Don's eyebrows rose. "Were you able to speak with Bob Mortenson?"

"We'll see him later today," Jeremy said. "We have some questions for you."

He held out the printed copies of the land investment deals that Vivian had managed to get off Kara's father's laptop, then laid them out on the desk for Don to look at.

"What can you tell us about these?" Kara asked.

Don put on a pair of reading glasses and bent over to look

at the papers. The reading glasses obscured the expression in his eyes. "Where did you get these?"

"Off my father's laptop."

Clearly surprised, Don glanced back at the papers and waved a hand. "Ancient history. I told you your father was friends with Bob. The two of them approached me about investing in these properties. We all made some good money from the deals. Didn't your mother tell you about this? The profits paid off the house you lived in."

That was news to her. "I thought the life-insurance money paid off the house." At least, that was what her mother had told her.

"One of the properties was zoned a natural resource area," Jeremy interjected. "How did you get around the designation?"

Don shrugged. "We filed the necessary paperwork, and the city rezoned it. Nothing nefarious about the deal."

"Can we see that paperwork?" he asked.

Her uncle's chin dipped. "That was over twelve years ago. You'll have to go to the records room and fill out a request. I certainly don't have any copies here." He folded his arms over his chest, then he patted his shirt pocket. "I almost forgot." From the pocket, he brought out the key chain with the turtle charm. "After you left last night, I found this in the sand near one of the sculptures." He held it out to Kara.

Pleased, she took the key chain. "Emily will be so happy." Kara put the trinket into the pocket of her suit jacket.

Don gathered the papers on his desk and held them out to Jeremy. "Now, if you'll excuse me, I do have a job to get back to."

Taking the papers, Jeremy said, "Thank you for your time, Don."

"Of course. Kara, can I see you and Emily again before

you leave? You can come to my place for dinner. Tomorrow night?"

As her uncle stared at her with an expected gaze, Kara couldn't say why she was hesitating. There was no reason for her to keep a distance from her uncle. Seeing him hadn't caused her grief to swamp her. Besides, he was all that was left of her family. She smiled her agreement. "That would be great."

She and Jeremy left Don's office and headed straight to the records room. Jeremy filled out the request forms, giving the dates indicated on the stack of documents he held.

The older man behind the counter made a face and warned them it might be a while before they could locate anything from that long ago. "We've only started digitizing records going back five years."

"Do what you can," Jeremy encouraged the man. "Anything would be appreciated."

Leaving city hall, Kara drove them off South Padre Island across the Queen Isabella Causeway through Port Isabel, home to the longest fishing pier in the state of Texas. Kara's father had taken her and the whole baseball ball team to the pier, known as Pirate's Landing Fishing Pier. That day had been filled with fun and laughter.

Sadness invaded her chest. "I miss my father."

Jeremy reached over and placed a gentle hand on her arm. "I miss him, too."

She slowed at a red light, and they shared a smile. For a moment, all she wanted to do was fall into his arms. Then a horn honked, bringing her attention back to driving. The light had turned green, and she stepped on the gas.

Forty minutes later, they were in the city of Brownsville, where the Mortenson Group had their office building. The company took up a whole floor in a newer high-rise. The receptionist at the front desk asked them to take a seat.

It wasn't long before a forty-something woman with dark red hair clipped back at her nape approached. She wore a light pink blouse and a bone-colored pencil skirt with matching high heels that clicked on the tile floor. Kara had never felt comfortable in heels.

With a polite and no doubt practiced smile, the woman stuck out her hand to Jeremy while totally ignoring Kara. "I'm Wendy Thompson, Bob's executive assistant. How can I help you?"

"Hello, Miss Thompson," Jeremy said politely. "Are you here to escort us to Bob's office?"

Wendy's smile faltered slightly. "I'm sorry—did you not receive a call this morning from our office?"

Jeremy gave a negative shake of his head. "No, I did not."

Wendy's eyebrows dipped with clear displeasure. Kara figured someone had dropped the ball and was going to get an earful from her.

She released a sigh that sounded like a cross between a huff and a grunt. "Unfortunately, Bob has come down with the flu. Most likely, he got it last night at the holiday event. I'm constantly telling him he needs to take precautions by washing his hands after going out in public. But you know, he has twin boys, and they're always coming down with colds."

"It seems convenient that he's sick," Kara said, drawing Wendy's attention. Was the man dodging them?

Wendy's pale brown eyes slid to her. "There's nothing convenient about it. I've had to reschedule all of today's meetings." Once again addressing Jeremy, she said, "Chief Hamilton, I will reschedule with you as soon as Bob is well enough. I hope you have a good day." With that, she turned and walked away.

"Do you believe he's really sick?" Kara asked as they headed back to the elevator.

"Hard to say. I already have a warrant in the works to search his office. I think I'll add his home to the request."

As slippery as Bob Mortenson was proving to be, she doubted he'd be careless enough to leave incriminating evidence lying around. "What are we hoping to find?"

"Anything that connects him to the recent murders and your father's cold case. My gut tells me they're all intertwined."

She let out a small half laugh, half scoff. "Let's hope the judge will sign off on the basis of your gut."

Jeremy shrugged. "Small town, remember? The current sitting judge likes me."

Kara liked him, too. He didn't take himself too seriously, and he hadn't let his position of authority go to his head. And he was so good with Emily. He cared about her safety. He was kind and gentle—and so handsome, even more so than when they were young. He'd filled out and matured in ways that set her heart pounding. She wondered again why he wasn't married with a family of his own.

The elevator doors opened, and Kara stepped inside. Jeremy followed and hit the button for the lobby.

As the elevator descended, Kara put her hand in her pocket and fiddled with the turtle charm. For some reason, having the little key chain close was like having a piece of her father with her.

As she played with the turtle, something on the charm snapped. "Oh no. I think I broke it."

She brought the turtle out of her pocket in two pieces.

Surprise arced through her as she realized the key chain was not in fact broken. The back half of the turtle concealed the body of a USB drive, and the top half served as a cap.

She held up the drive for Jeremy to see, and his eyebrows shot upward.

"Do you think that USB belonged to your father?" he asked.

"I have no idea. But we need to get to a computer to find out." She closed her fingers around the key chain and held it securely in her fist.

What would they find inside? And if it had been her father's, what secrets had he been keeping?

Back at the police station, Jeremy plugged the thumb drive into his computer. He had the inane thought that it looked like the turtle had dived head-first into the device.

For a long moment, nothing seemed to be happening. Suspecting that the drive was too old to connect to his updated computer, Jeremy reached to take the USB drive out but paused when the external drive icon popped up. Tensing with anticipation, he clicked on the icon.

"It's empty." Kara's voice filled with frustration.

Sharing her frustration, Jeremy hit Escape and then unplugged the USB drive. A thought occurred to him. "It could have been erased. I'm going to give this to Vivian. If there was anything on this at one time, she might be able to recover it."

Kara exhaled with a nod. "Good idea. If she's unable to recover any of the data that might have been on the drive, I can send it to the FBI technology group."

"Let's give Viv a chance first," he said as he led the way to the South Padre Island crime lab. "She's a genius at this sort of thing."

When they entered the lab, they found Vivian bent over a microscope, looking at something on a slide. She glanced at them. "Chief. You have something more for me?"

"I do." Jeremy placed the thumb drive on the counter next to Vivian. "I need you to see if you can recover any files off this. It appears to have been wiped clean."

Vivian straightened and took off her glasses. "Nothing is ever unrecoverable. People think deleting something actually deletes something. But there's always an electronic trace left behind." She picked up the thumb drive. "Half of a turtle?"

Kara held up the other half with the key-chain ring on it. "It was concealed inside this. It was my father's."

Vivian's smile was sympathetic. "I'll get right on this, but it may take a while. This looks old. I'll have to find the right device to do the recovery with."

Jeremy put a hand on her shoulder. "We appreciate it."

Once he and Kara were back in his office, he said, "I'm sure Emily must be missing you. Let's head back to my parents'. There's nothing more we can do here today."

"I can go on my own," she said. "You still have a job to do."

Was she trying to get rid of him? Old hurt surfaced, but he tamped it down. "As long as you're in danger, I'm not letting you go anywhere alone."

Hoping to lighten the mood, he added, "Besides, it's lunchtime. Mom texted to say she was making pizza."

"I saw the pizza oven in your backyard. Swanky."

"Mom and Dad love to make individual pies." His mouth watered just thinking about the homemade pizzas. "We need to get in on the action."

She flashed him a grin. "What are we waiting for?"

As they left, she worried the top half of the turtle key chain between her fingers.

He couldn't help but wonder what secrets the turtle concealed. And would the information lead them to Kara's father's killer?

* * *

Smoke from the stone pizza oven drifted on the breeze from the edge of the back patio, spreading the aroma of cooking meats and vegetables. Kara sat with Emily on a lounge chair as they waited for their pizzas to cook. In the chair beside them sat Julia, with Raz sitting between their chairs. Julia pet the dog as he kept his dark eyes trained on the horizon.

When Kara and Jeremy had first arrived back at the Hamiltons' home, they'd been ushered into the kitchen by Emily, who'd announced they had to build their own pizza. She'd proudly displayed her own creation of pepperoni, cheese and pineapple, to which Kara had added a few vegetables.

Kara's gaze tracked Jeremy now as he and Tarren helped Irene bring out several pizzas from the oven and lay them on the long table set up on the patio. She still couldn't believe she and her daughter were here, being included as if they belonged.

Her heart crimped with a yearning that she mentally shoved away. This was a temporary moment with the Hamiltons, and she decided to enjoy it while it lasted.

She smoothed a hand over Emily's soft hair. "We'll eat soon."

Emily grinned. "Smells yummy." She rummaged through her backpack for a hair tie. "Here, Mommy."

Taking the elastic band, she gathered Emily's hair and secured it at her nape.

"Jeremy mentioned the Mortenson Group."

Julia's words drew Kara's attention. "Excuse me?"

"The Mortenson Group," Julia continued. "I'm not sure what to make of them."

Kara perked up. "What do you mean?"

"They're one of our biggest supporters at the turtle sanctuary, but my boss was telling me that the Mortenson Group has been trying to buy the property the sanctuary sits on. So far, the board of directors has turned down their offers. But the amount keeps climbing. At some point, I fear the board will become bamboozled by the dollar signs rather than staying focused on the mission of the sanctuary."

"That's very concerning." Kara waved to gain Jeremy's attention. "Jeremy, over here, please."

Setting aside a pair of oven mitts and the wooden pizza peel, he hustled over. "Getting impatient for your lunch?"

Kara nodded to Julia. "Tell him what you just told me."

His sister repeated what she'd said.

Jeremy rubbed his chin as he seemed to digest this information. "Isn't the sanctuary property on protected land?"

Julia made a face. "Yes. But that doesn't seem to stop development. Just look at where the mall sits. It was once protected, too. 'Progress' is what they're calling it."

Rick stepped up with a nod. "It's true. Many on the city council want the island to grow and become more profitable. The Mortenson Group keeps petitioning the council to push back the natural habitat boundary. They even want part of the South Padre Island Birding, Nature Center and Alligator Sanctuary."

Kara hated to think of the picturesque bay-front boardwalks and swamps disappearing, not to mention displacing all the creatures that inhabited the section of the island.

"Dad, is the council going to allow it?" Jeremy asked.

Rick made a face. "Not as long as I've a seat at the table."

"Emily, your pizza's ready," Irene called out.

Slinging the backpack over her shoulders, Emily scrambled away and ran over to take the large plate from Tarren, who helped her find a seat at the long table. Once she was settled, he went back to helping Irene.

A deep, low growl emanated from Raz, and he stood up. His tail went straight in the air, his ears back.

From his place at the pizza oven, Tarren turned with his hand on his weapon. "He's alerting."

Before Kara could even stand, five masked men invaded the backyard and spread out. They were under attack.

THIRTEEN

Raz's fierce barks filled the air.

Fear for Emily flooded Kara's veins. Her daughter was sitting at the table, exposed and vulnerable.

Needing to get to her, Kara jumped to her feet but stilled.

Each of the masked invaders had a semiautomatic weapon in their hands.

They were outgunned. She met Jeremy's gaze and saw the same alarm reflected in his gold-flecked eyes.

Tarren gave low a command to Raz. Kara could only guess he was telling the dog to stand down because there were too many assailants. The barking ceased, but the dog remained poised to lunge at the closest masked man.

Emily, clearly scared, left the table and ran toward Kara.

A masked man grabbed her by the waist as she passed him, lifting her off her feet.

"No!" Horror flooded Kara's system, constricting her breathing and sending shivers of dread along her limbs. They had her baby.

Emily screamed and struggled against her captor.

Kara lunged forward but was blocked by two men who positioned themselves in front of her and Jeremy, their weapons aimed at their hearts.

"Give us the thumb drive if you want your daughter to

live." The nearest gunman stepped close. He was shorter than the others, but the automatic weapon in his hand was just as deadly.

"Mommy!"

Kara's blood ran cold at the sight of a gun pointed at her daughter's head. "I don't have it."

Jeremy took a step forward at the same time as Tarren. Raz shifted his focus to the man holding Emily. The two masked men held their weapons aimed at Jeremy and Tarren. The last gunman had the barrel of his weapon pointed at Rick and Irene.

"No sudden moves, Chief," the shorter masked man said. "We'd hate to mow down your whole family."

Jeremy slowly lifted his hand off his weapon, as did Tarren. "Don't hurt them." His voice held a warning.

"It all depends on how cooperative everyone is." The assailant gestured to Kara. "We'll take you then." He swung his gaze to Jeremy. "If you want them back, you'll give us the drive."

Kara backed toward Emily and the masked man holding her in the air. "I'll go with you—just let my daughter go."

"Just do as you're told, agent lady, and you'll both live." The shorter assailant grabbed Kara by the arm and propelled her toward the side of the house. The man holding Emily around the waist turned and hurried ahead of them. In an attempt to keep her daughter in her sight, Kara practically dragged her captor forward. She would do anything to protect her child.

She lifted a prayer that God would intervene. She trusted Jeremy would do what was necessary to get her and Emily back.

Out on the street, there were two black SUVs parked at the curb.

Emily was loaded into the back seat of the first SUV. Kara charged in that direction but the man behind her yanked her back and pushed her toward the second vehicle.

Digging in her heels, she demanded, "I have to be with my daughter."

The first SUV took off in a squeal of tires.

Panic lodged in Kara's throat. She couldn't lose Emily. "Wait!"

She flew into action, rearing her elbow back to connect with the diaphragm of the man holding the gun on her. Twisting, she went for a throat strike, rendering the man useless. His gun clattered to the ground as he crumpled, gasping for breath.

His fellow kidnappers rounded the corner of the house. Jeremy, Tarren and Raz were close on their heels.

Picking up the gunman's automatic weapon, she turned and aimed it at the three approaching masked men. "Drop your weapons."

The men skidded to a halt.

Jeremy and Tarren disarmed the gunmen and put them in cuffs while Raz moved to stand on the stomach of the assailant lying on the ground holding his throat.

"They took Emily." Kara couldn't keep the alarm out of her voice. She rattled off the license plate number of the SUV that had taken her daughter. "We have to get her back."

Using the radio attached to his uniform, Jeremy called for backup, then put out an alert on the SUV, giving dispatch the license plate number.

Kara ripped the mask from the head of the man on the ground. "Where are they taking my daughter?"

"I don't know," the man managed to squeak out through his injured throat. "We were paid a bunch of money to get the thumb drive. Taking her wasn't part of the plan."

"Shut up," one of the other suspects shouted.

"Where's the officer I had stationed out here?" Jeremy asked as he yanked the masks from the other men.

A brown-haired man with a beard gave a chin nod toward the bushes. "In there. He's alive."

Tarren ran to the row of shrubs. A moment later, he and the groggy officer emerged out of the tangle of foliage.

"Sorry, boss," the young officer said, rubbing the back of his head. "They came out of nowhere. Clocked me good."

Jeremy waved away his apology. To the assailants, he demanded, "Who's your boss?"

The assailants remained silent.

"We need a lawyer," a dark-skinned man finally stated. "We'll only talk to you with a lawyer."

Jeremy growled in response.

Despair invaded Kara's chest. How had she let this happen?

A text dinged on her phone. She dug it out from the pocket of her suit jacket.

Her heart thudded. "It's from the kidnapper. He says if I want to see Emily alive, I must bring the thumb drive to Gravity Park." One of the island's amusement parks.

Within moments, more South Padre Island police cruisers screeched to a halt in the street in front of the Hamiltons', the vehicles' lights flashing the neighborhood with blue and red.

After handing over the assailants, Jeremy said to Kara, "Let's go get Emily back."

"We don't have the thumb drive," she reminded him.

"We'll stop by the station to get it. She's more important."

Kara wanted to kiss him but instead hustled to the rental car which was closer than Jeremy's SUV.

He held out his hand for the keys. "I'll drive." Without

hesitation, she tossed him the keys. She was too nervous to be behind the wheel.

"We'll follow you," Tarren said as he and his K-9 ran past them. "I have Emily's sweater. Raz can track her at the park." He secured Raz in the back compartment of his police vehicle before climbing into the driver's seat.

Kara was thankful she had these men at her back. She'd never been on the victim side of a kidnapping before. She'd worked many cases where she'd come in and profiled the kidnapper. She needed to do that here, but at the moment her brain wasn't functioning.

All she could think about was her daughter being in danger. Emily had to be so scared. It was all Kara could do not to scream with rage.

Jumping into the passenger seat of the rental, Kara swallowed back the bile of fear surging into her throat as she hung on to the door handle.

Jeremy drove like a race-car driver through South Padre before bringing the sedan to a skidding stop at the front curb of the police station. Tarren brought his vehicle to a halt beside them.

Hating that time was ticking by so quickly, Kara jumped out of the vehicle and raced alongside Jeremy into the police station while Tarren and Raz waited outside.

Vivian was not in the crime lab. Despair gripped Kara. Where was she? They needed the thumb drive.

Taking her hand, Jeremy pulled her toward a back office. The lights were on. He pushed open the door without knocking.

Vivian sat at her desk, typing on her computer. Her gaze lifted. "Impatient much?" She rose to her feet with the thumb drive in her hand. "I managed to recover the files. I've emailed them to you."

"Thank you so much." Grateful to have the means necessary to get her daughter back, Kara snatched the thumb drive, turned and ran toward the exit.

"We need the USB now. I'll explain later," Jeremy shouted back to Vivian as he caught up to Kara. They both rushed to get into the rental car.

The ping of Kara's phone announced the arrival of another text. Heart thumping wildly, she looked at it. "It says to go to the mini-golf course."

Jeremy's hand grasped hers. "We'll get her back."

She squeezed his hand. "Jeremy, I'm really scared."

"I know. Me, too." He started the car and hit the gas.

A burning sensation built in Kara's chest. But words wouldn't come. She let out a moan as a prayer burst out of her mouth. "Please, God, please don't let anything happen to Emily. I beg of You, let us find her. I don't need closure if that's not in Your plan. Just let my baby girl be okay."

"Amen," Jeremy said as he slowed the vehicle and turned into the amusement park entrance. Tarren's vehicle was right behind them.

The place was bustling. How were they going to find Emily? There were so many civilians, so many potential victims.

A security guard sauntered forward. His pinned-on name tag read *Calvin*. "You can't park here."

Jeremy flashed his badge. "We have a hostage situation. We need to get to the mini-golf course."

Calvin's eyes widened. "Should I have the park evacuated?"

"No—" Kara and Jeremy said simultaneously.

"This is a sensitive situation, and we don't want to cause anyone to panic." Jeremy needed everyone, including the criminals, to stay calm. Emily's life hung in the balance.

Calvin blinked and then gestured. "This way."

They left the car and hustled after Calvin, who wound them through the festively decorated park toward the far end. Kara didn't see Tarren or Raz, but she knew they wouldn't be far behind.

The mini-golf course was a popular attraction. A line had formed of people waiting their turn to step onto the green turf with their golf clubs and brightly colored balls. Upbeat Christmas music played over hidden speakers.

"What can I do to help?" Calvin asked.

"Find a place to stay out of sight, but keep us in your line of vision," Jeremy told him. "I may need backup."

Calvin nodded eagerly and backed away before turning and hurrying behind the mini-golf kiosk.

Kara stared at her phone, willing the kidnappers to communicate. Her nerve endings were on fire as anxiety raced through her body.

Jeremy slipped the thumb drive into her hand. "Hold it up. They could be watching us."

She pinched the thumb drive between her fingers and held it up high in the air as she turned in a slow circle, making sure that the device could be seen from every angle.

A dark flash off to the left had her gaze zeroing in on Raz. The dog halted a few feet away and hunched down next to Tarren, who stood behind a popcorn vendor.

Kara's gaze snagged on a man dressed as Santa in a red velvet outfit, black boots and a white wig and beard. He was handing out candy canes to children and their parents as he maneuvered through the crowded park.

Santa worked his way over to where Jeremy and Kara stood.

Wary, Kara pivoted to keep Santa in her view.

He held out a candy cane. "I was told to exchange the candy cane for something else?"

Fisting her hand around the USB port, Kara demanded, "Where's my daughter?"

Despite the painted-on rosy cheeks, Santa frowned. "I don't know anything about your daughter. I was paid a hundred bucks to walk over here and give you this." He waved the striped candy stick in her direction. "And you're supposed to give me something."

Jeremy discreetly flashed his badge at Santa. "Then what are you supposed to do with it?"

Santa's eyes rounded and his big shoulders rose. "I'm supposed to give whatever you hand me to someone behind the Ferris wheel."

Kara's gaze sought out the large, moving wheel lit up with Christmas lights in red, green and white. All the gondola cars were filled as the machine rotated on a fixed stand. Who was waiting there for the thumb drive?

Jeremy moved away to use his radio, no doubt to tell Tarren about this new development.

Kara hesitated. If she handed over the thumb drive, her daughter would be returned. Or so the text said.

But could she trust whoever had taken Emily?

If she didn't hand it over, would they really harm her daughter? Was she even here?

From her peripheral vision, Kara saw Raz and Tarren leave their position. The dog moved with purpose toward the mini-golf course, and the pair disappeared from sight deep into the attraction's maze of putting greens.

Was Raz on Emily's scent?

Kara lifted another prayer, asking God to please let Tarren and Raz find her daughter.

"Do you have something for me or not?" Santa insisted as he handed out candy canes to a passing family.

Keeping a tight hold on the thumb drive, she asked, "How were you contacted, and when?"

"Some dude," Santa said. "About five minutes ago."

"What did he look like?"

"Big, ugly, his arm was in a sling," Santa replied.

Jeremy joined them. "Maybe the guy I winged who tried to kidnap you the other day from the van?"

How did that help them now? Kara's phone dinged again. This time, the text's instructions were to hand over the USB to Santa, or Emily would get a bullet in the head.

Shaking from the adrenaline and fear coursing through her veins, she passed the phone to Jeremy and then handed over the thumb drive to Santa.

He slipped the device into the pocket of his red pants and moved away.

"Get down!" Jeremy yelled at the exact moment she noticed a red dot on her chest.

Jeremy tackled her, taking her to the ground. A bullet whizzed past her head, slamming into the concrete behind her. If he hadn't shoved her to the ground, it would've gone through her heart.

Scrambling, Kara and Jeremy took cover behind a cotton-candy vendor. All around them, people screamed and ran in every direction.

After a several moments, the world quieted. The criminals had ceased firing. Jeremy and Kara slowly, cautiously broke cover. No more shots rang out. Did that mean the suspects had received the thumb drive and left? Where was Emily?

"Mommy!"

Kara turned to see Emily in Tarren's arms as he and Raz rushed over from the mini-golf course.

"Raz found her in a tunnel," Tarren said as they approached. "He tracked her scent from the sweater. She was bound and gagged. But she's okay."

Overwhelmed with relief and joy to see her child unharmed, Kara took Emily into her arms.

Jeremy waved to the security guard who hustled over.

"Stay with them," he told the young man. "Keep them safe."

Calvin nodded and took a stance in front of Kara and Emily while Jeremy and Tarren raced to the Ferris wheel and disappeared around the backside of the amusement park ride.

Holding Emily close while keeping an alert eye out for any threat, Kara thanked God for her answered prayer. Her daughter was safe.

Anger at the men who did this bubbled in her chest. Kara vowed to bring the people responsible for her daughter's kidnapping to justice.

Jeremy returned empty-handed.

"The shooter's gone. Tarren will stay and continue searching." He put a hand on her shoulder. "Let's get you two out of here."

Disappointed but not surprised that the suspect fled, she nodded and shifted Emily on her hip. Sandwiched between Tarren and Jeremy, with Raz at his handler's side, they swiftly left the amusement park.

But Kara feared this wasn't the end of the danger. What would the people who took the thumb drive do when they realized the device had been wiped? And if they didn't have the resources to reclaim the data, would they come after her and her daughter again?

Instead of going to the Hamilton home after several hours at the police station, Kara had insisted on securing a hotel room. She didn't want to put the Hamiltons in any more danger, and she needed a place that she could control. A place that would be less traumatic for Emily.

Kara had requested a room on the tenth floor overlooking the ocean, and Jeremy provided police protection. Officer Stacy Ridgefield was stationed outside the hotel room door, with more officers at each end of the floor.

All night, Kara debated whether she should take Emily and return to Virginia or continue to seek answers to her father's murder. Leaving might be the safer thing for them both. But then she'd always be looking over her shoulder, and the abductors might still follow them there. She needed to put an end to this. She needed Jeremy's help.

Now, in the light of day, the thought of leaving was stronger. She wanted nothing more than to whisk her daughter to somewhere they would be safe. But until she and Jeremy discovered who was after her and why, Kara wasn't sure there was such a place.

Julia had arrived a few moments ago and declared she was staying with Emily so that Kara could meet with Jeremy downstairs.

Kara had called him as soon as she'd awakened and told him she wanted to continue with the investigation. From his tone, she'd known he wasn't a fan of the idea, but she'd insisted. She was an FBI agent, and though most of her profiling work was done from the periphery of a case, she was trained and motivated to bring this chapter of her life to a close.

"Are you sure?" Kara felt bad that Julia was taking time out of her own life to be here. "Don't you have a job you're missing?"

"Of course I'm sure. I'm taking vacation time." Julia's smile was filled with reassurance. "We'll be good here." She snuggled with Emily on the king-size bed. "We're going to find the Disney Channel and watch—"

Emily had the remote in her hand. "Princesses," she burst out.

"Yes, and maybe Mickey Mouse or some other cartoons that I have no idea about...but will one day need to know."

Kara arched her eyebrows. "Really? Are you planning to start a family right away?"

"I'm not getting any younger," Julia quipped with a grin. "Besides, after spending all this time with this munchkin, I've got a yearning." She put a hand over her heart.

Though Kara had never experienced that longing prior to having Emily, she understood it now. She sent up a quick prayer that God would bless Julia and Tarren with children. Had anyone asked Kara five years ago if she'd wanted children, she would have said she was perfectly content with her life as it was. But now that she had her daughter, she was amazed by the depth of love that a human could feel for another, along with an ache of dread that something might happen to her. Parenting wasn't for the faint at heart.

Remembering how Tarren and Raz had discovered Emily inside one of the mini-golf course tunnels with her hands and feet tied together and a gag over her mouth still had the power to make Kara's blood run cold.

She was thankful the kidnappers hadn't hurt her, but there was no telling what would have happened had the situation gone south.

Stifling a shudder, Kara reminded Julia, "Officer Stacy will be right outside the door."

Julia and Emily looked at each other and then back to her.

"Mommy, Peace Officer Stacy should come watch cartoons with us."

Indulging her daughter with a smile, Kara gestured toward the door. "We'll have to ask her."

Kara figured it would be okay if Stacy were in the room since there were officers positioned at both ends of the hall and downstairs near the elevators. Jeremy had said he wouldn't take any more chances with Emily's life. And Kara believed him.

She couldn't imagine going through this without him. How was she going to walk alone again?

Acid churned in her gut. That was a problem for another day.

She picked up her backpack-style purse and opened the door to the hall. Stacy stood outside and smiled a greeting.

"These two want you to come and watch cartoons with them," Kara said, holding the door open for her.

Stacy shook her head. "The chief said I was to stand guard."

Kara nodded. "You can just as easily stand guard inside the room as outside the room."

Stacy glanced inside, and Kara followed her gaze. Julia and Emily waved her in.

"If you're comfortable with it," Stacy said.

"I trust you," Kara told the other woman. "It's not often I say that to anyone."

"I'm honored."

Stacy slipped into the room and Kara shut the door behind her. She waited a beat until she heard the dead bolt lock, and then she flipped the hanging sign to Do Not Disturb.

Laying a hand on the door, she said a quick prayer before taking the elevator to the lobby, where she met Jeremy.

He stood near a water fountain feature. Tall, muscled and so handsome.

She had to admit she liked the way his police uniform fit as well as the tender smile on his face as she approached.

Her heart skipped a beat. Whew.

She really needed to find her professional detachment.

But this was Jeremy. Her first love. And now her backup. Or maybe she was his. Either way, she needed to get a grip and stay focused on the task at hand, which was finding out who was behind the attacks on her. Mooning over her past love wasn't productive nor smart.

"I just got off the phone with Wendy at the Mortenson Group," Jeremy said. "The search warrant has been served and is in progress. Bob's livid, but he's available to see us."

"Good. Let's see what he has to say."

Jeremy put a hand on her arm, and his touch sent a ribbon of awareness through her. "You know, no one would blame you if you decided to take a step back. I can handle this."

Covering his hand with her own, she stared into his eyes. "No way, Hamilton. You know I don't back down from a fight."

His mouth lifted at the corners. "Oh yeah, I know."

She hoped and prayed they'd have the answers she needed to close her father's cold case before Christmas. Because as the holiday drew closer, so did the danger.

FOURTEEN

The moment Kara and Jeremy stepped into Bob Mortensen's office on the twentieth floor of his towering building in Brownsville, he exploded at them. "I came in when I heard what was happening. Your people have been here all morning searching our offices. What do you hope to find?"

Jeremy didn't take the bait. Men like Mortenson thought they could intimidate others because of their power and position. "What do you have to hide?"

Bob lifted his hands. The gold-and-diamond cuff links caught the light. "Nothing. I demand you tell me what this is about."

"We'll get to that," Jeremy said. "I have to inform you that I have officers on their way to your home to serve a search warrant."

Bob's face darkened, and his skin turned molten red. "This is outrageous. I'm going to call the mayor." He reached for the phone on the desk.

"I assure you it's all on the up and up," Jeremy told him. He laid out the photographs of the four dead men who had been found in the past week and a half on the island. "What can you tell me about these four men?"

Bob barely glanced at the images laid out before him, but he removed his hand from the phone and straightened.

"Is this some kind of scare tactic? Are you accusing me of something?"

Interesting that that was where his mind went.

"Take a look," Jeremy urged.

Beside him, Kara stepped closer. Her finger tapped against the last photo of Anthony Kubaik. "This man was driving one of your trucks."

Bob sent her a disdainful glare before his gaze dropped to the pictures on the desk. "That may be. I don't know all of my employees. We employ over a thousand workers throughout the state of Texas."

"These men are on your payroll, then?" Kara stated.

Bob's gaze snapped up. "That's not what I said. I have no idea if these men are in my employ. You'll have to ask HR."

"Oh, we will." Kara laid out copies of the property deal that Bob, her father and her uncle had been involved in. "Do you recognize these?"

For a long moment, Bob stared at the documents. "Where did you get these? They're private. You shouldn't have them."

Jeremy crossed his arms over his chest. "You do recognize these documents. They have your signature on them."

"Of course. These are land deals I did years ago." His gaze zeroed in on Kara. "With your father, I might add. He's the one who brought the idea to your uncle and me."

Jeremy slanted a glance at Kara. Don had said that Bob and Paul had approached *him*.

Her gaze narrowed. "That's not the way my uncle tells it. And my father's not here to defend himself now, is he?"

The hard expression etched on Bob's face suddenly softened. "Your father's death was a blow to us all."

Kara stiffened. "He was murdered."

"Nasty business," Bob said. "But what does that have to do with me? Wasn't he found on the baseball diamond? Shouldn't you be looking at a disgruntled student or a teacher from the high school?"

"Oh, we're turning over every rock." Jeremy's gut was telling him the man was deflecting way too much.

Bob spread his hands. "You won't find anything here or at my house."

Kara retrieved another set of documents from her purse—the ones that had been recovered from her father's thumb drive. She laid them over the other documents. "What about these?"

Bob scowled and bent to look at them closer. "What are these?"

Jeremy was sure he heard a hint of panic in the man's voice.

"My father was working to block the development on the land where the mall is because it was part of the natural preserve."

Bob straightened. A hard gleam entered his gray eyes. "If that's so, I didn't know about it. You should be talking to your uncle. He and your father were thick as thieves."

Kara took a step forward, and Jeremy placed a hand on her shoulder. The last thing he needed was for her to create a situation where Bob claimed harassment. It was bad enough that as soon as they left his office, Bob would call the mayor and the mayor, in turn, would call Jeremy.

"Thank you for your time, Mr. Mortenson," Jeremy said. "We'll head to HR now to find out about your employees."

"Alleged employees," Bob said between clenched teeth. "If they did something wrong, it had nothing to do with my company or me."

"Whatever they were into got them killed," Kara said.

His eyes widened. "I didn't know. I hope you find whatever you're looking for."

Somehow, Jeremy doubted the man's sincerity as he gathered all the documents up from the desk. "We'll be in touch."

In the hall, they met with Wendy, who told them HR was on the next floor down. They got into the elevator.

"That man's hiding something." Kara's voice seethed with anger.

"I agree, but we can't push too hard until we have more information or evidence of wrongdoing."

"I don't like how he talked about my father."

The elevator dinged, and they stepped out onto the floor below Bob's office and headed to the HR department. Jeremy's phone rang. They paused while he answered. "Chief Hamilton."

"Chief, I'm calling from the city zoning records department regarding the paperwork you put in a request for," the man on the line said. "Unfortunately, I realized the documents you wanted are gone. You see, there was some sort of water damage about ten years ago, and that whole section of our records room was destroyed."

"Convenient." Jeremy breathed out. "Thank you for checking."

He hung up and relayed the information to Kara.

She shook her head. "We seem to be getting blocked at every turn. Does Bob have that much power in this town?"

They headed into the HR office. The fifty-something woman behind the desk smiled. "Chief Hamilton. Wendy said you were headed down. I've been instructed to tell you that the warrant you have doesn't include employee personnel documents. We can't release any information without a warrant specific to our employee records."

Why wasn't he surprised? He tempered his voice to keep the frustration and anger from showing. "Then we'll be back."

They returned to the elevator and pressed the button for the lobby.

"What's Bob hiding?" Kara stepped into the elevator car. "Does it have anything to do with my father? Why would he have anything to do with the death of his employees?"

"All good questions that we'll find answers to eventually." He sent up a silent prayer that that was true.

The elevator stopped halfway down the building. When the doors slid open, a large man in a navy suit with a shaved head stood there, his arm held in a black sling.

The man from the van. The one Jeremy had shot. And the man who'd allegedly asked Santa to collect the USB drive.

Reacting instantly, Jeremy blocked the elevator door open with a foot, reached for his weapon and growled, "Police. Stay still. I want to talk to you."

Kara withdrew her weapon as well. "FBI."

The man pivoted away from the open elevator and ran down the hall, hitting the stairwell door with a bang.

They raced after him. He swiftly descended the stairs.

Keeping him in sight, Jeremy, with Kara on his heels, took the concrete steps two at a time. The man exited the stairwell on the ninth floor.

With caution tripping down his spine, Jeremy paused, pushed open the door and peeked around the corner.

The man stood in front of the elevator at the end of the hall, frantically pushing the buttons.

The elevator dinged. The doors slid open, and he stepped inside.

In tandem, Jeremy and Kara raced down the hall, but the doors had slid shut by the time they reached the elevator. The arrow light indicated the elevator was going up.

They had no way of knowing which floor the man was aiming for as the elevator had no number display.

"He has to work for Mortenson." Kara called the elevator again.

Jeremy agreed. "Let's find Bob and ask."

They entered the car and pushed the button for the Mortenson floor. The elevator rose past the floor that the Mortenson Group was on and kept going.

Jabbing the button for the next level, Jeremy's breath caught as the car didn't respond but kept going up.

"I've got a bad feeling about this." He pushed all the buttons, even the emergency stop.

When the elevator finally halted, the whole button panel lit up.

"We have to get out of here." She pulled the emergency alarm. Nothing.

The car squeaked as if the weight was too much for the cables.

Jeremy dug his fingers into the rubber piping along the doors and attempted to pull them apart. To no avail.

The service hatch wasn't an option because it was bolted shut with access only from the outside by a maintenance key or by the fire department. He checked his phone. No bars inside the elevator. His radio produced only static.

Kara grabbed a hold of one end of the handrail. "If we can get it off the wall, we can use the flat edge to pry the doors open."

Admiring her innovation, he grabbed a hold of the other end of the elevator railing, and together they pulled. But it held. "We need to unscrew the bolts."

He didn't have anything on him that would do the trick.

Kara shrugged off her backpack. She dug around inside until she produced a multipurpose Swiss Army knife. "I've learned a few things from you. Always be prepared."

She worked on the bolt on her side and handed the tool

over to Jeremy. Soon they had both bolts unscrewed and the railing came away from the wall.

The elevator slipped several feet, sending them both crashing to the floor.

It stopped abruptly. No doubt the emergency brakes on the car had engaged.

He helped Kara to her feet. "You okay?"

"Yes." Her tone was tinged in fear.

Without wasting any time, they wedged the flat end of the railing between the rubber casing of the elevator doors. Together, using their combined strength, they managed to pry the doors open to find the floor at eye level.

Using the railing as a fulcrum between the two sliding doors, Jeremy turned to Kara. He threaded his fingers together and made a basket. "Step up. Get out."

She tossed her backpack through the opening onto the floor above them. "You first." She made a basket with her hands.

He frowned. "Kara, this is not the time for you to compete."

She held his gaze. "*You* first. Then you pull me up. I can't pull you up."

Hating that she was right, he put a hand on her shoulder and stepped into her hands. He gripped the edge of the floor and lifted himself up with her help. Once he was out of the elevator, he scrambled to turn around and leaned over on his belly.

His arms reached for her. "Hurry. I don't know how much longer the brakes will hold."

The car squeaked and fell another inch.

Jeremy's heart jumped into his throat. "Kara."

She reached up to grip his forearms. He gripped hers. She kicked off her shoes and, using him as leverage, walked up the elevator door until he could grasp her beneath the arms. The elevator squeaked.

She was half in and half out.

If the elevator dropped, she'd be cut in half.

Lord, please.

Terror sliced through Kara. Half of her body hung over the ledge of the floor, into the elevator. Any moment, the elevator could drop out from under her, and she'd... A shudder ran through her. She tightened her hold on Jeremy's arms to aid his attempt at rescuing her. Her feet clawed at the wall.

His muscles bunched as he let out a growl and yanked her from the elevator's clutches.

Her hips banged against the ledge, the pain barely registering.

A loud, resounding snap echoed in her ears, followed by a shrill alarm.

She tucked her knees and pulled her feet out of the elevator car just as the entire thing plummeted to the bottom of the shaft, landing with a cacophony of noise and debris. The whole building shook.

Kara clung to Jeremy, her heart pounding in large booming beats.

Jeremy's hands framed her face. "Are you hurt?"

Her mind tried to make sense of what just happened. "No. But that—"

His lips sought hers. She clung to him, thankful to be alive. Thankful to this man for rescuing her from the clutches of death. Thankful to God for His and Jeremy's protection.

She savored the closeness, the way he calmed her heart despite the rapid beat of the muscle. Kissing Jeremy felt right, natural, and every fiber of her being wanted to stay wrapped in his embrace.

Tears pricked her eyes.

She chalked up the chaos of emotions to the near-death experience and the ebb of adrenaline.

The kiss eased, and they drew away from each other.

She stared at him, memorizing his face. Wishing they were somewhere else and that their futures could be intertwined.

But she couldn't stay on South Padre Island. And she didn't even know if he felt the same pull that drew her to him, the same pull she'd felt years ago. Only it was strong now, more intense and yet so painful because ultimately she wasn't sure she could trust he wouldn't hurt her heart again.

All around them people came out of their offices and filled the hallway.

"What happened?" a woman asked.

"It was the elevator!" a man exclaimed.

"Was anyone hurt?" another woman asked.

Quickly, Kara disentangled herself from Jeremy and they both rose.

Drawing Jeremy away from the crowd, now staring at the empty elevator shaft, Kara spoke to him in a low voice that shook with relief. "This was no accident. I'm sure Bob Mortenson or the guy with the arm sling had something to do with the elevator dropping."

Jeremy's expression took on a fierceness that was both surprising and yet warranted. He was angry. So was she.

He cupped her elbow. "Let's go have another chat with Bob."

They stepped into the stairwell and had to jostle past people flooding the stairwell hoping to escape. No doubt people feared the building was going to collapse. The thought sent a tremor racing along Kara's limbs. She sent up a prayer the foundation would hold.

When they reached the Mortenson Group floor, they found

Bob's executive assistant directing people down the stairs. The relentless blaring of the building's alarm echoed through Kara's brain, making her head ache.

"Where's Bob?" Jeremy asked Wendy.

"He went out the private exit as soon as you left." She pointed upward. "There's a helipad on the roof. He's already in his helicopter by now."

Jeremy huffed out a breath. "Do you know where he's going?"

"Did you see a guy wearing an arm sling?" Kara asked at the same time.

Wendy frowned. "No to both questions." She gestured for more people to move into the stairwell.

Shifting to stay out of the way of the exiting employees, Kara asked, "Is Bob alone?"

Wendy shrugged. "He usually has a bodyguard. But I haven't seen Dwight today."

"Is Dwight a big guy with wide shoulders and a buzz cut?" Jeremy asked.

"A big guy with wide shoulders," Wendy replied. "Not sure about the buzz cut. But could be. He usually has dark curly hair and a mustache."

Could it be the same man? The description wasn't much to go on, but it was all they had.

Kara pressed, "What's his last name?"

Wendy frowned. "Flores."

"Where's the security office?" Jeremy asked.

"In the parking garage." She gestured toward the stairwell. "We really should evacuate. The build could come down any second."

Kara shared a glance with Jeremy, and they seemed to be in sync. Without needing to speak, they pushed into the stairwell and moved quickly through the evacuating crowd. Their destination: the security office, where Kara hoped they'd find footage of the elevator sabotage.

They had to go out into the lobby to find the stairwell to the basement parking garage. Emergency personnel were directing people to the exit doors and out onto the sidewalks.

Jeremy showed his badge to a Brownsville officer. "Who's in charge?"

"That would be Captain Levinson." The young officer pointed to an older uniformed gentleman with gray hair who was consulting with the fire department chief.

Jeremy and Kara hurried over and explained their theory that the elevator dropping was not an accident.

"We want to look at the building security footage," Kara told the man, flashing her badge along with Jeremy.

"What's the FBI's involvement in this? Are you working a case?" Captain Levinson asked.

"We're working a case," Jeremy supplied, saving Kara from answering. "Agent Evans-Mitchell is consulting with the South Padre Island police."

Captain Levinson nodded. He pointed to a door behind the reception desk. "We'll take the stairs."

They followed the captain down the stairs to the basement garage parking area, where they found the security office. It was empty.

No doubt the security guards fled when the elevator landed.

Kara sat down at the bank of monitors. Her fingers flew over the keyboard. There were no cameras in the elevator shaft. She figured out how to rewind the security footage of the lobby, hoping to get a glimpse of the man with the sling.

A man roughly the same size and height with one arm in a sling had walked through the main doors not long after Kara and Jeremy arrived, but his face was a round, glowing orb.

Captain Levison gestured to the monitor. "What's happening here?"

"I've seen this before," Kara said. "He has some sort of device around his neck that reacts to the video cameras. There was a bank robbery a few years ago where the suspects used the same method to disguise their faces."

"We've seen his face," Jeremy said. "Even without the video, we can identify him."

"But we need an image to send out to all law enforcement agencies." Kara turned in her chair. "A forensic artist. The Bureau has one. I can reach out."

"No need," Jeremy said. "Stacy is our department's forensic artist. And she's good."

Respect surged through her. "Like I've said, you're always prepared."

Jeremy flashed her a grin.

Her stomach clenched as she returned the smile.

Then Jeremy thanked Captain Levinson before putting his hand on her lower back. The warmth of his touch spread through her, offering comfort and yet setting off a buzz in her blood.

She was falling for him all over again. At the moment, she struggled to resist and attributed the struggle to the brush with mortality.

They left the building. Thankfully they had parked down the block and weren't trapped inside by the fire department and emergency vehicles.

They headed back to South Padre and the police department.

Jeremy's phone chirped. He put it on speaker. "Hamilton here. I've got you on speaker, Daniel."

"Hey, boss. We're at the Mortenson home. There's something here you need to see."

Kara met Jeremy's gaze as he said, "We're on our way. Text me the address."

Within a moment, his phone dinged with an incoming text.

Kara grabbed the phone and directed him to the Mortenson home.

The large estate just outside of Brownsville was massive and oppressive in scope. They passed through an open gated entrance and drove toward the Mediterranean-style sprawling mansion. The white stucco home had many floor-to-ceiling windows beneath its red-tiled roof. Palm trees swayed in the breeze of the ocean. Manicured lawns stretched around the building.

"Obviously, Bob has done well for himself," Kara said.

"At the expense of others, no doubt," Jeremy added as he parked beside two police cruisers, one from South Padre Island and the other a Brownsville police vehicle. A white van with the South Padre Island Police Department logo on the side was parked at an angle.

"Vivian beat us here." He gestured to the South Padre Island Crime Unit van.

Kara's stomach twisted with acid. Was money the motive for her father's murder? She made a mental note to run her parents' financials along with her uncle's and Bob's. Her father had tried to block the development of a piece of property that Bob and Don had been eager to build on.

That had to be the reason why her father had been killed.

But who killed him? Bob Mortensen...or her uncle Don?

The acid burned its way to her throat at the thought of her mother's brother being involved. And what was her mother's involvement?

And how did her father's murder relate to the other recent murders? Were those four men somehow in on the deal as well? They would've been very young at the time, but it wasn't outside the realm of possibility.

Why did someone pay George Watkins to try to kidnap her? Why did the other armed men go to such lengths to try to nab her, the bat and the thumb drive?

Today, and during many other attempts, someone had tried to kill her.

Was it because they thought her father's secrets would die with her? What did anyone have to gain from hurting her?

She glanced at Jeremy. It wasn't just her today that they'd tried to kill. Had they hoped if they killed Chief Hamilton, the investigation into her father's murder would cease?

The questions bounced around her head like a ball in a pinball machine.

Daniel met them out front of the massive double wooden doors.

"We didn't find anything in the house." He led them toward the garden.

Falling into step with him, Jeremy asked, "Did you find something buried in the garden?"

"No, sir, we found a wood chipper," Daniel explained. "Mrs. Mortenson claims it belongs to their gardeners. They were clearing some bushes off the property."

"Sounds plausible," Kara said as they trudged through a bed of roses toward a large mechanical device.

Vivian was scooping up wood chips from a small pile and putting them into evidence bags.

"What did you find?" Jeremy asked.

"Birch chips." She held up the bag. "Look around you. Do you see any birch trees?"

Kara made a quick visual search. Then her heart rate ticked up. "The bat used to kill my father was made of birch."

FIFTEEN

Kara's words echoed through Jeremy's brain. Her bat, the bat they suspected was used to kill Coach Evans, was made from birch. And there wasn't any birch on the Mortenson property visible from where they stood.

Focusing on his crime scene tech, Jeremy asked the question burning in his mind and hoped for a positive answer. "Vivian, if there was blood on those chips, can you pull DNA off them?"

"I believe so," Vivian said. "I'm going to take it all to the lab, and we'll see what we can extract. I'll call you as soon as I know anything."

Encouraged by Vivian's response, Jeremy's gaze went to the back porch. Mrs. Elise Mortenson stood watching with her twin boys. She was dressed like she was heading to a fancy party, in a silky cream blouse and matching linen pants, and her twins wore matching starched shirts and navy slacks. "I think we need to have a talk with Mrs. Mortenson."

"Maybe she'll know where her husband has gone." Kara strode toward the back porch stairs.

Jeremy gave his officers instructions to find Dwight Flores and take him into custody on suspicion of kidnapping and attempted murder, as well as put an alert out for Bob Mortenson under the same charges. He also made a call to Stacy, checking up on his sister and Emily.

"Everything is good here," Stacy told him. "We were thinking about heading to the pool."

Jeremy hesitated. There was no reason to believe that Bob Mortenson or his bodyguard Dwight, or whoever the man with the injured arm was, would go after Emily again. But he didn't want to take any chances. "I'd prefer you all stay in the room. When Kara and I return, we can accompany you to the pool."

"I'll pass the message along," Stacy said. "Not sure the little girl's going to be too happy."

As much as he didn't want to disappoint Emily, it was for her own good. "When we get there, we're going to need your artist's skills."

"Of course. I actually brought my bag with me," she replied.

Jeremy hung up and joined Kara and the Mortensons. He couldn't interpret the look on Kara's face as he joined them.

He caught her attention. "Everything okay?"

"I'd like to speak to Mrs. Mortenson alone," Kara told him, her gaze not wavering.

Taking that as his cue to entertain the twins, he said, "Boys, walk with me."

"I don't think—" Elise Mortenson began.

But Kara held up a hand. "It will be fine. They'll stay within eyesight."

Elise gave a clearly reluctant nod.

Jeremy herded the twin boys off the porch and into the garden. Though he was curious, he realized how much he trusted Kara and had every confidence she knew what she was doing.

A warmth spread through his chest. He trusted she'd get

answers. His respect for her as an FBI agent nearly matched his admiration and affection for her as a woman and a mother.

He was falling for Kara a second time.

Oh man, he was in deep trouble.

"Where did you get the bruise on your arm?" Kara asked once the twins were out of earshot.

When Mrs. Mortenson had been gesturing and protesting the invasion of police in her home, the sleeve on her silk top had ridden up, revealing the purple telltale signs of a fresh bruise.

Elise tugged the sleeve down. "I don't know what you mean."

Classic behavior of battered woman syndrome—denial and covering up. "I'd prefer you didn't lie to me," Kara told her. "I saw the finger imprints. Somebody grabbed you hard."

"I fell," Elise insisted. She turned and walked away, heading over to an outdoor seating area. She took a seat and crossed her ankles. Her linen pants fluttered in the slight breeze that had kicked up.

"Elise, you're being abused." Kara joined her. "I recognize the signs."

Elise's gaze stayed on her sons. "My husband will be very angry when he realizes I let you onto the property."

"You didn't let us," Kara said gently. "You had no choice. But you do have a choice now. Your husband is abusing you. I can help you."

Elise frowned. "You don't know my husband. You don't know what he's capable of."

Unfortunately, Kara had some ideas.

Four—possibly five—deaths had been connected to Bob Mortenson. Her father maybe included.

Kara's heart squeezed tight.

Deciding to veer the conversation away from the sensitive topic of domestic abuse for now, she said, "Do you know Don Kearns?"

Elise gave Kara a side-eyed glance. "He's one of my husband's friends."

"Friend? Not business associate?"

With a shrug, Elise said, "Maybe. They often meet behind closed doors in my husband's study."

Don had made it seem as if her dad and Bob had been the ones who had been friends. While Bob had said it was her father and Don who were close.

But now Elise was saying Don and Bob were not only friends socially but met in private meetings here at this house. Why had Don been less than forthright about his relationship with Bob? What was her uncle hiding?

"Did you know Coach Paul Evans?" Kara asked. Her heart lodged in her throat as she awaited the answer.

Shaking her head, Elise said, "No. I didn't meet Bob until long after the coach's murder."

"So you're from the area?"

Elise shook her head. "South Carolina."

Raising her eyebrows, Kara said, "Then how do you know about the murder?"

This time, Elise faced Kara. "It comes up every year on the anniversary. Whenever we go into South Padre Island, people talk about it. They say someone got away with murder. There's speculation that the person still lives on the island or close by. But no one knows who."

A lump formed in Kara's throat. People still remembered her father's murder. She hated that his legacy was tragic violence. Did anyone remember him as a great coach?

She remembered the wonderful father he'd been to her and all the young people he'd met.

She swallowed and took a breath before managing to say, "Does Bob believe the murderer is still around?"

Small creases appeared between Elise's blond brows. "I couldn't begin to guess what Bob thinks."

"Your husband was apparently a friend of my father's," Kara said.

Elise turned to her. "Who's your father?"

Forcing words past the dryness now invading her mouth, Kara said, "Coach Evans."

Elise's eyes widened. "The coach was your father?"

"Yes."

Empathy lit her brown eyes. "You must've been, what? Sixteen?"

"Seventeen," Kara said. "Just shy of my eighteenth birthday."

Sympathy played across Elise's face. "That must've been rough to lose your father at that age. I can't let my sons lose their father. They need him. Boys need their fathers to grow up to be men."

"How long do you think it will be before Bob turns his anger from you onto your boys?" Kara watched her closely. "If he hasn't already?"

Elise took in a sharp-sounding breath. "He would never hurt them. He adores them."

"For now," Kara insisted. She'd seen similar scenarios numerous times. "But once they become rebellious teenagers? My guess is he won't have patience for them."

The other woman's shoulders slumped. "I'll protect them."

"At your own expense," Kara said with certainty.

"What does it matter to you?" Elise snapped.

A fierce protectiveness had her hands fisting. "I don't like anyone being hurt by somebody bigger and stronger."

Tears pooled in Elise's eyes. "He has a hair trigger. He doesn't mean to do the things he does. He just—"

"Rages."

"He promises—"

"Empty promises." Kara gentled her voice to say, "Let me help you and your kids get away from him. At least until we're done with this investigation."

She spread her hands. "Where would we go? He has resources all over. Bob has powerful friends."

"I'm not afraid of powerful people." Kara took her hand. Elise was so thin and fragile feeling. "The FBI have safe houses that he would never be able to find."

The ringing of a phone somewhere in the house had Elise sitting straight up like somebody had poked her in the back. "That's him."

Kara cocked her head. "How can you be sure?"

"He's the only one who calls that phone." She jumped to her feet. "And if I don't answer it…"

Kara stood and gestured to the house. "Then you better answer it. Find out where he is. But don't let on that we're here."

Walking behind Elise, Kara noted how stiff and tense the other woman was as she moved into the house. Elise headed for the desk in what could only be called a man cave. The large space overlooked a lap pool in the side yard. Kara found the room oppressive with its dark wood paneling and deep brown leather furniture.

She gazed with interest at the sports memorabilia and other very expensive collectibles displayed, as if Bob Mortensen needed the public presentation of wealth to remind himself who he was or what he'd accomplished.

Elise picked up the receiver of the vintage phone on the desk. "Hello?"

Kara crowded close to her, grasped the old-fashioned telephone handle and tilted it so she could hear.

"The police are there. You shouldn't have let them come in." There was no mistaking the disdainful tone of Bob Mortenson's voice.

A spasm of fear crossed Elise's face.

Kara patted her shoulder and made a gesture for her to keep talking.

"I had no choice," she said. "Where are you?"

"You think I'm going to tell you with that FBI agent standing next to you? You're even dumber than I thought."

Elise gasped and fumbled to hold onto the receiver.

Kara's gaze searched for a hidden camera. Her gaze landed on a Model T airplane. The propeller didn't look quite right.

"Wave to the camera," Bob said. "You're not going to pin anything on me. You're not going to get the chance."

The line went dead.

Dread invaded Kara's chest. Tension tightened the muscles of her shoulders. A quake in the pit of her stomach moved like a tidal wave through her. His words replayed through her head. *You're not going to get the chance.*

They had to get out of the house.

Elise dropped the receiver. It clattered against the desk. "He's watching us. Oh, no. You said you can help us—"

Cutting her off, Kara grasped Elise with an arm around her waist and propelled her out of the house and down the porch stairs. The other woman's heels had her stumbling when they reached the grass.

"Everybody, run!" Kara yelled at the top of her lungs. "Bomb—"

The house exploded, the force sending her face first into the ground.

* * *

"Kara!"

Jeremy's panicked yell barely registered through the ringing in Kara's ears from the house exploding behind her. She spit out the dirt that had ended up in her mouth when she'd face planted on the lawn. She flopped onto her back and stared at the plumes of smoke filling the Texas sky. It seemed like she was constantly being laid out flat on her back. She didn't like it one bit.

Turning her head, she met Elise's gaze. The other woman rolled to the side. Dirt and grass now stained her white outfit and smeared her makeup.

Moments later, Jeremy was in Kara's line of sight. He was bending over her, touching her, his mouth moving as he said words she couldn't hear through the ringing.

He gripped her shoulders and got into her face. "Are you hurt?"

Between reading his lips and the muffled words she could make out she was pretty sure she understood his question. "I don't think so. Was anyone hurt?"

She could barely hear her own voice. She reached up to tug at her ears. It helped bring the world back into sensory focus.

"No. Everyone else was far enough away," he replied.

She closed her eyes and sent up a prayer of thanksgiving that no one else had been close enough to the blast to be harmed. Of course, Bob had no idea if anyone else besides her and his wife would have been blown to bits. Or did he?

Pushing herself upright on her elbows, she took stock of her situation. She and Elise had been catapulted several yards from the house. She searched for hidden cameras, but with the smoke and the debris, it was hard to tell.

Jeremy captured her attention by cupping her face and kissing her.

Surprise arced through her. And relief quickly had her kissing him back. She reveled in the feel of his lips pressed to hers, his strong, capable hands holding her in place.

Aware of the audience around them, she said against his lips, "Jeremy."

He broke the kiss to press his forehead to hers. "You scared me."

This time she heard him, even though it sounded like he was far from her despite being only inches away.

Her heart bumped against her ribs.

Knowing he cared nearly brought tears to her eyes. She remembered the boy he'd been, but the man he'd become was so much more appealing. He was thoughtful, protective and compassionate. Yet he was brave and not afraid to show vulnerability.

What more could a woman want? What more could *she* want?

Everything. But she knew that wasn't possible. The hurts of the past were a wedge between them. She still didn't understand why he thought she'd broken up with him when he'd been the one to stop communicating.

Jeremy helped her to a full sitting position. "What happened?"

"Bob Mortenson called," she told him. "He said something about not being given a chance to catch him."

She'd believed he was going to blow the house up. And she been right.

Kara turned to look again at Elise. Her perfectly coifed hair had come loose. She was holding her wrist awkwardly against her chest as her boys gathered around her. They were all crying, tears streaming down their faces.

Kara was glad the boys weren't harmed. But from the looks of it, Elise was injured.

"Help her," she said to Jeremy.

He frowned and waved for others to come forward. Many had taken cover but were now collecting at the edge of the lawn.

Within moments, an ambulance was on site. Apparently, someone had already made the call. It wasn't long before Kara was checked out by the paramedics, as was Elise.

As Kara suspected, she had only minor cuts and mostly soft-tissue damage. Elise's wrist was broken from landing on it. The paramedics wrapped it and put her in the back of the ambulance.

Jeremy placed his hand on Kara's lower back and nudged her to start walking. "Let's get you out of here. We can't sift through the debris until the fire department gives the all clear. And there may be more explosives rigged around the house."

Knowing that was true, she leaned into him as they moved in tandem a safe distance away from the house.

"We have to get Elise and the boys into protective custody," Kara told Jeremy before the ambulance could leave. "Bob's abusing her. He just tried to kill her. And me."

And almost succeeded. Next time, would he finish the job?

SIXTEEN

Jeremy nodded as he assigned an officer to accompany Elise and her boys to the hospital.

After the ambulance left, he said, "I can have them taken to the police station after Elise's wrist is set and put in a cast."

"That's a temporary solution," Kara said. "I'll contact the local FBI office in Corpus Christi and have Elise and the twins stashed in a safe house."

"That works," Jeremy replied.

"He was watching us." She shuddered with the memory. "There was a camera hidden in a model plane in the study. He no doubt has cameras all over the house. He's a control freak."

"We'll get him," Jeremy vowed. "We'll monitor every means of transportation out of Texas."

"He's far from here by now," she said. "I can have him put on the FBI's most wanted list. He'll slip up. A narcissist like him won't last long in the shadows."

But he could lead them on a merry chase. She had to know what happened with her father and to keep Emily safe. "We need Vivian to run that DNA test on the wood chips ASAP. If the results come back with a match to my father, then we'll know for certain Bob was somehow involved in my father's murder."

"True. However, the evidence would only prove the stolen bat ended up on his property. Someone else could have brought it here to use the wood chipper."

The reminder of how the bad guys had crashed into Jeremy's police vehicle and pushed them into the ocean sent a shiver through her. Trapped in the SUV with the water rapidly rising had been terrifying. Not to mention being punched in the face.

She pushed the memory away. "Knowing what a control freak Bob is, he'd have known if someone else had been on his property doing his bidding."

"We do have him dead to rights on attempted murder of a federal agent," Jeremy continued. "No matter what, he's going down."

"Yes, and maybe we can make a deal for information on my father's murder. Or get him to confess." The questions of how her mother and her uncle were involved lingered in her mind. "But we still can't connect Bob to the deaths of his employees."

"Something will turn up. If we can bring his bodyguard in, we'll get him to flip." Touching her arm, he said, "I'll tell Vivian to make testing the DNA on the wood chips a priority."

Appreciating how he seemed to know what she needed to hear, she took his hand and threaded her fingers around his. It felt right to hold on to him. Not caring that others were watching, they headed to the crime scene unit van.

They stopped to talk to Vivian, explaining the urgency of the DNA testing on the wood chips. She promised to do it right away.

Then Jeremy opened the passenger door of Kara's rental car. Grateful to slide into the passenger seat, she rested her head against the headrest.

Once Jeremy was behind the wheel and driving them away from the Mortenson estate, she said, "There's still so many unanswered questions. Why was someone trying to kidnap me, and now why are they trying to kill me? And is Bob behind it all? Or just this latest attempt?"

"And who killed the four Mortenson Group employees, and why?" Jeremy voiced more questions. "What does it have to do with Bob and his company?"

"And how deep is my uncle involved? What do you think Bob meant when he'd told us to talk to Don? And was my mother involved?"

Kara's fists clenched.

She hated thinking her mother had had anything to do with her father's death, but the baseball bat had been found in their home, a house she'd refused to sell. Because she was harboring the weapon used to kill Kara's father? To what purpose?

Kara rubbed at her temples, where a headache born of frustration throbbed. "Emily and I are supposed to have dinner with Uncle Don tonight."

"I strongly suggest you cancel." Jeremy's voice held a concerned note.

"I could," she began, but an idea formed. "Or better yet, you could come with me. I'll leave Emily with your parents, Tarren, Raz and Julia, because there's no way I'm putting her in danger again."

For a moment, Jeremy was quiet. Then he said, "All right. We need to do more digging into your uncle and his connection to Bob Mortenson so we are armed with information that can't be dismissed."

"There has to be someone we can interview who was on the city council twelve years ago." Her mind whirled with all the unanswered questions. "Someone must remember how and why the Mortenson Group was allowed to build on land that was once deemed protected. I have a feeling that's why my father was killed—he was trying to block the building on the land. Bob could have paid someone to take him out to pave the way for the project."

But that didn't explain how the baseball bat had ended up in her mother's trunk in the attic of her childhood home.

"We'll talk to my father," Jeremy said. "He's on the city council now. He can find out who was around back then."

"Good. We have a plan." She liked plans. She liked having things lined up. She didn't like the ambiguity of unanswered questions and unknowns. But without looking Bob Mortenson in the eye, she really couldn't know his motivations or who else was involved.

Until then, she needed to confront her uncle. He knew something more than what he'd let on. She was determined to get answers, no matter how painful they proved to be. Because until she had the closure she sought in her father's cold case—she glanced at the man beside her—and in her relationship with Jeremy…there was no way she could leave the island and this chapter of her life behind.

Staring at Stacy's composite drawing of Dwight Flores, Jeremy was satisfied with the likeness and sent it out to all law enforcement agencies.

Dwight would not go unnoticed for long.

After a stop to have a chat with a couple of former city council members, Jeremy drove Kara to her uncle's apartment building in his personal vehicle. It would be a while before the South Padre Island police SUV could be replaced. He parked at the curb, giving himself plenty of room in case they needed to exit quickly.

When they were on the sidewalk, Kara paused before opening the building's entrance door. "Do you mind if we take the stairs?"

He chuckled, totally on board with not getting in an elevator anytime soon. They took the stairs and came out on Don's floor. Kara marched up to the door and knocked.

A moment later, it opened.

Don's eyes widened as his gaze bounced between Kara and Jeremy. "I was expecting you and Emily. Why did you bring the chief?"

"Don't be rude," Kara said, her tone filled with irritation. "Jeremy and I need to talk to you. Without little ears."

Don visibly reined in his attitude and gave a very polite smile. "Of course. Come in."

Jeremy wondered if the man aspired to go into politics. He certainly had the suave, practiced veneer down pat.

Don's apartment had a high ceiling, plush white carpet and bone-white leather living room furniture. A square dining table with four cushioned high-back chairs sat before a floor-to-ceiling window with a stunning view of the Gulf of Mexico.

"I hope you like chicken Parmesan." Don gestured to the table set for three. "I thought I would pick something that a four-year-old would enjoy."

"She would have," Kara said. "But we have some questions before we eat dinner."

He scowled and gestured to the living room. Light from the canned overhead light glinted off the gold Rolex on his wrist.

Kara perched on the edge of the couch cushion. Jeremy would have preferred to stand but felt he needed to show solidarity to Kara, so he sat next to her.

Don took a seat in an armchair.

Kara rolled her shoulders before she said, "Uncle Don, do you know where Bob Mortenson has gone?"

Dropping his chin, he shook his head. "Why would I know where Bob is? I would assume he's home with his family at this time of day."

"No, he's not." Annoyance vibrated through her voice. "Did you know he was abusing his wife?"

Frowning, Don made a face. "That's news to me."

Jeremy didn't think his disgust was manufactured. "Why didn't you tell us that you and Bob went before the city council twelve years ago and pressed the issue of converting the natural preserve area where the mall is into buildable land?"

Shifting his gaze from his niece to Jeremy, Don said, "I don't know what you're talking about."

Kara made a noise of disbelief. "Uncle Don, we talked to two city council members right before we came here who were on the board back then. Why are you lying?"

Jeremy wanted to know what else he was lying about.

Don's nostrils flared. "I wouldn't say we pressed," he said, his voice tight. "We made a request. The city council voted to allow it. Nothing illegal happened."

Kara spread her hands. "But why didn't you tell us?"

He shrugged. "It didn't seem relevant."

Rolling her eyes, she said, "Did you know my father was trying to block that development?"

He heaved a heavy sigh. "I did. And I sided with him. But then he was murdered."

Jeremy didn't see the correlation. "Why did his murder change your mind?"

Don slanted his gaze toward him. "I only agreed with Paul because he was married to my sister. When he was gone, I decided not to stand against progress."

"You mean you got scared." Kara met Jeremy's gaze before turning back to her uncle. "Do you know who killed my father?"

Don's hands flexed on the arms of the chair. "If I did, I would have turned them in."

"How did the bat that was used to kill my father end up in my mother's house?" Kara's voice was strained.

Don's Oxford-encased toe tapped against the carpeted floor. "I don't have an answer for you. And unfortunately, my sister is gone, so she can't tell us why she hid the bat in the attic."

Jeremy tilted his head. Neither he nor Kara had mentioned that the murder weapon had been found in the attic. There was only one way he would know where the chest that held the bat had been in the house. "You put the bat there."

Don's whole body radiated agitation. "What are you accusing me of?"

Kara bolted to her feet, her hands fisted at her sides. "You had something to do with my father's murder."

The apartment's front door burst open.

Bob Mortensen and his bodyguard, Dwight Flores, crowded into the apartment. Both were carrying semiautomatic rifles, the barrels of which were aimed at Jeremy and Kara.

Realizing the situation was going south quickly, Jeremy stepped in front of Kara and turned his back to the men to conceal what he was about to do.

Kara leaned to the right to peer around him.

Jeremy jammed his hand into his pocket to grab his phone and pull the device out far enough to unlock it with his thumb. He touched the phone icon, hit Tarren's name in his favorites and left the line open.

"Turn around. Get your hands in the air," Bob demanded.

Carefully, Jeremy let the phone slide down his leg and drop soundlessly to the carpet. With the toe of his boot, he kicked the device under the couch as he turned with his hands raised above his shoulders. He prayed Tarren would hear what was happening and show up.

Kara moved to stand beside him and raised her hands.

Don, his expression exasperated, turned to Bob. "What are you doing here?"

Bob's mouth stretched into a semblance of a smile. "Tying up loose ends."

Turning toward Kara, he said, "Okay, FBI lady. You're right—your uncle is lying. He stashed the bat in your mother's house."

Kara sucked in a sharp breath as the implications of what Bob just revealed ran through her system. Obviously, he'd heard the last part of their conversation as he and his minion had busted into the apartment.

She narrowed her gaze on her uncle. "You killed my father?"

Don shook his head vigorously. Contrition marred his brow. "No. I didn't. You were correct about your father wanting to block the mall development."

"He had no vision," Bob groused.

Sending him a withering glare, Don continued. "We met him at the baseball diamond that Sunday morning to try to convince him to let us proceed. When he told us that he would do everything he could to keep us from building there—" Don pointed a finger at the other man.

Kara's gaze zeroed in on the high-priced watch encircling his wrist. Now that she knew her uncle was complicit in her father's death, she wondered if this could be the missing timepiece.

"Bob killed Paul in a fit of rage," Don continued, his voice dripping with contempt. "He grabbed the nearest bat and swung. And kept swinging. I tried to stop him but it was too late."

She closed her eyes against the image his words provoked.

"I didn't mean to do it," Bob said, though his voice held no remorse. "And then your uncle took the bat...and has been blackmailing me ever since."

A deep rage welled within her, but she knew she had no play here, not against the weaponry held by Bob and Dwight. She could draw her weapon and fire, but not without risking being hit in return. Acid churned in her gut.

She hoped whatever Jeremy had done with his phone meant backup was on the way.

Jeremy said, "What about your employees? Four of them are dead. Did you kill them, too, in a fit of rage?"

Bob sneered. "They were stealing from me. The three of them thought they were being clever and had a cunning plan to take from me what was mine. They didn't know I had eyes everywhere."

"What about Anthony Kubaik?" Kara asked. "He was in the truck that rammed into us." Her gaze darted to Dwight. "You were, too. Which of you slugged me?"

Bob gestured to Dwight, who had remained silent this whole time. "Ask him."

Kara's focus moved to the big man. "Well?"

"Anthony punched you." Dwight swung his glare at Bob. "His death was on your orders. He knew about the bat, and you wanted him silenced."

"That's right," he gloated. "You're a sheep, just like everybody else. But you're my sheep."

Without warning, Dwight swung the weapon away from Kara and Jeremy toward Bob. "I'm nobody's sheep."

Bob gave a dismissive shrug. "But you're paid handsomely. And you take my money. I'll pay you double what I offered you before if you point that at those two." He flicked his hand. "Get rid of them."

Dwight returned his aim to Kara and Jeremy.

Kara stepped closer to Jeremy and took his hand. She didn't want to die tonight. She had to live for Emily. They needed to come up with a plan on how to get out of this situation.

Maybe if she could keep Bob and Don talking it would give her and Jeremy an opportunity to fight their way out of this. Or more time for help to arrive.

Though she knew the truth now about her father's murder, there was still more she needed to uncover.

Her gaze locked on her uncle. "Is that my father's watch?"

He put his hand over the timepiece, and his lips pressed together before he said, "Yes. I didn't want it to get lost or stolen. I'd always meant to give it back to Laine but..."

Her fists curled. "Was my mother aware of what happened to my father? How was she involved?"

Don's face spasmed. "She didn't know. I convinced her to take you and leave town. I told her I would see to the care of the house. And every time she mentioned selling it, I told her it wasn't a good time."

Kara's knees nearly buckled with relief to know that her mother hadn't been duplicitous about her husband's murder.

"Why were you trying to kidnap Kara?" Jeremy asked, his attention on Bob.

He shrugged. "I wasn't sure how much she knew about me or if she knew where the bat was. I was sick of being blackmailed."

"You had my homes searched," she said. "But you didn't know about the attic space."

Bob's lip curled. "No." He shot a glare at Dwight. "No one looked there."

Movement at the corner of her eye had her stiffening. Was that Raz crawling across the floor? She saw a shadow at the door. Tarren?

Hope flared within her chest. Backup had arrived.

Jeremy gave her hand a squeeze, then released her to step toward the window, drawing the other men's attention away from the front door. "So, what's the plan, Bob? You're going to kill us. And Don, too? Is he a loose thread as well?"

Bob laughed, and the sound shivered along Kara's spine. "I'm done being blackmailed. My life here on the island is over. I'm taking my money and running."

"There's nowhere you can hide," Jeremy said, taking another step away from Kara toward the window.

She didn't know his plan, but she readied her body to move. The question was, in which direction?

Then everything happened at once.

Raz lunged from his position on the floor, latching on to Bob's arm holding the gun. Bob screamed, and the gun fell to the carpet.

Tarren tackled Dwight from behind, taking him down to the floor. Jeremy quickly disarmed him.

Several South Padre Island police officers rushed through the open door.

Don vaulted toward a sideboard.

Kara raced across the room, grabbing his hand just as he reached for the gun inside the top drawer. "I don't think so. You're done, Uncle Don."

With satisfaction, she placed cuffs around his wrists and allowed one of the police officers to escort him out of the apartment. Other officers took Bob and Dwight away.

A wave of dizziness washed over Kara. It was over. The cover-up of her father's murder was finally out into the light.

Jeremy folded Kara in his arms.

The adrenaline letdown had her wrapping her arms around his waist and pressing her cheek to his heart. She finally had the closure she needed. She could let her father's memory rest in peace.

She glanced up at Jeremy. There was still more they needed to wrap up. "I want to look at that shoebox."

The grim set of Jeremy's mouth had her tensing. Did he not feel the reconnection that she did? Did he want her to leave?

Hours later, after booking Bob, Don and Dwight for murder, attempted murder and various other charges, Jeremy stopped by his apartment to retrieve the shoebox.

Was she going to stick to her mantra that the past had to stay in the past? He had to believe that they could deal with what was behind them so that they could have a future together.

Because he didn't think he could survive her leaving him again. Not when his heart was fully hers, now and forever.

Kara sat on a lounge chair out on the back patio of the Hamiltons' home and watched the waves push toward the shore. The moon was full and bright. The cooler night temperature soothed the anxiety cresting inside of her.

After giving her statement at the police station, she'd picked up Emily at the hotel and brought her back to the Hamiltons'. She and her daughter both needed some tender care. She'd put Emily to bed and answered as many questions as she could from the Hamiltons before claiming to need some air as she waited for Jeremy to bring the shoebox.

Needing to be honest with herself, she admitted she loved Jeremy—probably always had and always would. But she'd suppressed the emotion because of hurt. She'd let bitterness and anger take root all those years ago.

How could Jeremy think she'd been the one to break off their relationship?

What would be revealed in these letters? Could she handle this trip down memory lane?

She had to. She couldn't let the past haunt her and keep her from moving forward anymore.

The sliding glass door behind her opened.

She glanced over her shoulder to see Jeremy step outside and stride toward her. He'd changed into slacks and a long-sleeve shirt. His hair looked freshly washed and his jaw clean shaven. So handsome.

He held the shoebox in his hands.

Anticipation revved in her blood, increasing the nervousness thrumming through her veins. "Hey."

"Hi." He sat down next to her and offered her the box. "These are all of our exchanges after you left town. The last one is on top."

She clutched the box to her chest, unsure she wanted to relive those memories. But she had ventured this far into the past. Plus, she wanted to prove that she hadn't told him to leave her alone. He had to have misinterpreted whatever it was she'd said. She needed to make him understand how she felt then and now. "Thank you."

She removed the lid of the box and took out the stack of printed emails and note cards she'd sent him. "It's too dark out here."

"I can take care of that problem." He stood and moved to plug in the overhead garden lights that bathed the patio in a warm glow.

She took the top folded piece of paper and set it aside. She would get to it soon enough. Starting at the first email he'd printed out, she read her way through the stack with her heart lodged in her throat. She'd loved him so much. And with each email or note, she recalled his response. The memories were bittersweet.

Then she read the last email he'd printed out.

Her breath stalled in her lungs.

He was right.

The note said in no uncertain terms that she needed him to leave her alone because he was too painful a reminder of what she'd lost. She needed to move on with her life without him. And that he should do the same.

She pressed the printed paper to cover her pounding heart. For a moment, dizziness threatened to topple her right out of the chair. Taking deep breaths to regain her equilibrium, she held up the note. "I did *not* write this."

He cocked his head. "It has your name on it. Plus, it has the date and your email address in the corner."

"It does. But I'm telling you I didn't type this email."

A deep suspicion swept through her, making her nauseous.

A frown marred his forehead. "If you didn't, then who?"

"There's only one explanation." She hated to even think about it.

For a moment, he held her gaze.

Her pulse quickened.

The tenderness flooding the depths of his brown eyes made her want to weep.

They both knew who had written the email.

"My mother," she said softly. "I can only assume she was afraid I'd come back here and stay when she refused to return."

Jeremy gathered her close, and she laid her cheek against his chest.

He leaned back and held her gaze. "I'm so sorry. I should've known you hadn't written it," he said, his voice thick with emotion that could only be described as regret and self-recrimination. "I should've demanded an explanation face-to-face. I should have fought for you. For us."

Sorrow for the time lost filled her with regret, and fresh tears streamed down her cheeks. "If you had come, life would've been different for us."

Then she gave him a smile that wobbled at the corners despite her best effort to be strong. "But I have Emily. We both have careers we love. None of that would have happened if you..."

How could she regret David and Emily?

Jeremy smoothed back her hair and caressed her face. "If I'd been brave enough to face you."

This wasn't all on him. "Or if I'd been brave enough to stand up to my mother and return here to find out why you'd stopped writing."

She nuzzled her face into his palm and cherished the feel of his touch. "We can circle the drain all night on past regrets and hurts, but ultimately, we have to decide how to move forward."

Her heart thumped hard against her ribs as she met his gaze. "Jeremy, I want a second chance. A do-over."

She touched his face. "I love you, Jeremy Hamilton."

Joy spread over his handsome, dear face. "I love you, Kara. I always have. I want to make a family with you and Emily, if you'll have me."

Delight burst through her as she slid her arms around his neck. "Of course I'll have you, Hamilton. Yes, please. This will be the best Christmas ever."

He grinned right before his lips captured her mouth in a heart-melting kiss.

"Mommy?"

With an embarrassed smile, Kara turned to find Emily, Irene and Rick standing a few feet away.

Irene and Rick beamed with clear surprise and pleasure.

Jeremy eased away from Kara and drew her to her feet.

"Sorry," Irene said, sounding anything but. "She couldn't sleep and wanted to find you."

Opening her arms, Kara said, "I'm right here."

Emily ran the short distance, and Kara swept her up into her arms. "Honeybee, what would you think of spending Christmas here with the Hamiltons?"

"Can we? Yay!" Emily clapped.

Irene and Rick joined in the applause.

Then Emily placed one hand on Kara's cheek and reached her other hand for Jeremy. He indulged her by stepping closer and encircling Kara's waist with his arm.

Emily placed her hand on his cheek. "Christmas kiss!"

With her heart nearly overflowing with love for her child and this family, Kara was happy to oblige her daughter's request. She leaned over and kissed Jeremy.

EPILOGUE

Jeremy watched as his sister and his best friend exchanged vows in front of their families and friends. His heart swelled with love and pride. How had he never seen how good these two were together until danger had threatened their lives?

Julia looked like a princess in her white wedding gown, and Tarren cleaned up nicely in his tux. Raz sat at Tarren's heels with a black bow tie around his neck. His dark coat had been brushed to a sheen, and he seemed proud to be in the front of the assembly.

Across the aisle, standing in the bridesmaid line, Jeremy met his soon-to-be bride's gaze. Holding a colorful bouquet that spoke to the beauty of spring, Kara was lovely in a floral dress that swished around her knees. Her dark hair had been swept up in some fancy do that exposed the creamy column of her neck. He itched to place a kiss on the tender skin.

He couldn't wait to be the ones standing at the altar so they could begin their future.

Kara smiled with love shining in the purple-tinged blue depths of her eyes and winked at him. His grin widened.

She'd transferred from the FBI office in Alexandria, Virginia, to the one in Corpus Christi. However, she was planning on taking leave after their upcoming nuptials in June. They wanted to give Emily a sibling as soon as possible, and they would live in Kara's childhood home. The place was getting a makeover and a second chance at providing Kara new memories to take into the future.

With a tilt of her head, Kara directed Jeremy's gaze to where Emily, dressed in a matching flower girl dress, sat on his father's lap holding a colorful stuffed turtle from the Safe Haven Turtle Sanctuary, given to her by Julia with a promise to see the baby turtles as soon as it was nesting season.

Happiness fairly glowed off his parents. Both had tears in their eyes. They were increasing their family.

As the pastor announced Julia and Tarren husband and wife, Jeremy sent up praise to God above for all the blessings of a life filled with second chances and an abundance of love.

* * * * *

If you liked this story from Terri Reed,
check out her previous Love Inspired Suspense books:

Standing Watch
Trained to Protect
Search and Detect

Available now from Love Inspired Suspense!

Find more great reads at www.LoveInspired.com.

Dear Reader,

I hope you have enjoyed this journey with Kara and Jeremy as they carved out a path through the past by bringing to light disturbing secrets and forged a new future together in *Texas Christmas Cover-Up*.

Kara was determined to wall off the past, but ultimately, she confronted her pain and grew to where she could learn and accept what had been and look forward to what could be. While Jeremy had closed off his heart, believing doing so would keep himself from getting emotionally hurt, a reunion with his former flame rekindled the fires of love and allowed him to take the risk of welcoming Kara and her daughter into his life.

It was also a grand time bringing back characters from *Trained to Protect*, the previous book set on South Padre Island. Writing a suspense story set at Christmastime is always a challenge. We want those cozy, feel-good moments to relish the holiday spirit, but we also want the heart-pounding action and danger to keep us on the edge of our seats.

I hope you have found all of this and more between the pages of this book.

If you'd like to learn more about me and my books, visit my website at www.terrireed.com, and sign up for the newsletter for updates on my writing and my life and fun ways to receive book mail.

Until next time,
Terri Reed

Get up to 4 Free Books!

We'll send you 2 free books from each series you try PLUS a free Mystery Gift.

FREE Value Over **$25**

Both the **Love Inspired®** and **Love Inspired® Suspense** series feature compelling novels filled with inspirational romance, faith, forgiveness and hope.

YES! Please send me 2 FREE novels from the Love Inspired or Love Inspired Suspense series and my FREE gift (gift is worth about $10 retail). After receiving them, if I don't wish to receive any more books, I can return the shipping statement marked "cancel." If I don't cancel, I will receive 6 brand-new Love Inspired Larger-Print books or Love Inspired Suspense Larger-Print books every month and be billed just $7.19 each in the U.S. or $7.99 each in Canada. That is a savings of 20% off the cover price. It's quite a bargain! Shipping and handling is just 50¢ per book in the U.S. and $1.25 per book in Canada.* I understand that accepting the 2 free books and gift places me under no obligation to buy anything. I can always return a shipment and cancel at any time by calling the number below. The free books and gift are mine to keep no matter what I decide.

Choose one:
- ☐ **Love Inspired Larger-Print** (122/322 BPA G36Y)
- ☐ **Love Inspired Suspense Larger-Print** (107/307 BPA G36Y)
- ☐ **Or Try Both!** (122/322 & 107/307 BPA G36Z)

Name (please print)

Address   Apt. #

City   State/Province   Zip/Postal Code

Email: Please check this box ☐ if you would like to receive newsletters and promotional emails from Harlequin Enterprises ULC and its affiliates. You can unsubscribe anytime.

Mail to the Harlequin Reader Service:
IN U.S.A.: P.O. Box 1341, Buffalo, NY 14240-8531
IN CANADA: P.O. Box 603, Fort Erie, Ontario L2A 5X3

Want to explore our other series or interested in ebooks? Visit www.ReaderService.com or call 1-800-873-8635.

---

*Terms and prices subject to change without notice. Prices do not include sales taxes, which will be charged (if applicable) based on your state or country of residence. Canadian residents will be charged applicable taxes. Offer not valid in Quebec. This offer is limited to one order per household. Books received may not be as shown. Not valid for current subscribers to the Love Inspired or Love Inspired Suspense series. All orders subject to approval. Credit or debit balances in a customer's account(s) may be offset by any other outstanding balance owed by or to the customer. Please allow 4 to 6 weeks for delivery. Offer available while quantities last.

Your Privacy—Your information is being collected by Harlequin Enterprises ULC, operating as Harlequin Reader Service. For a complete summary of the information we collect, how we use this information and to whom it is disclosed, please visit our privacy notice located at https://corporate.harlequin.com/privacy-notice. Notice to California Residents – Under California law, you have specific rights to control and access your data. For more information on these rights and how to exercise them, visit https://corporate.harlequin.com/california-privacy. For additional information for residents of other U.S. states that provide their residents with certain rights with respect to personal data, visit https://corporate.harlequin.com/other-state-residents-privacy-rights/.

LIRLIS25